PRAISE FOR THE UNSEEN WORLD SERIES

"This is an amazing book filled with magic, consequences, and what happens when you fight rather than turning away. This is Omelas, for magic. This is the price that must be paid. This is the story the others forgot to tell."

—Fran Wilde, award-winning author of *Updraft* and *Horizon*.

"Strong characters and a captivating revenge plot make this a fun, absorbing read for those who like their magic, and their magicians, dark and twisty."

—*Kirkus*

"The characters and the Unseen World flourish in her gorgeous prose."

—*Publishers Weekly*

"Imagine the dueling club in Harry Potter all grown up and out for blood."

—*Shelf Awareness*

"Howard's magical world is wonderfully vivid; the magic itself engages all the senses, making each spell feel tangible. The disturbing, thrilling, and lovely moments pulse with striking language, and the fast-paced story is polished with a bit of humor that helps keep the novel light and fun. This riveting book is perfect for readers who want to escape."

—*San Francisco Book Review*

"A really good book. Its characters come vividly alive, its prose is precisely observed; and it's both tense and incredibly compelling."

—*Locus*

Also by Kat Howard

The Unseen World Series

An Unkindness of Magicians

Roses and Rot

A Cathedral of Myth and Bone

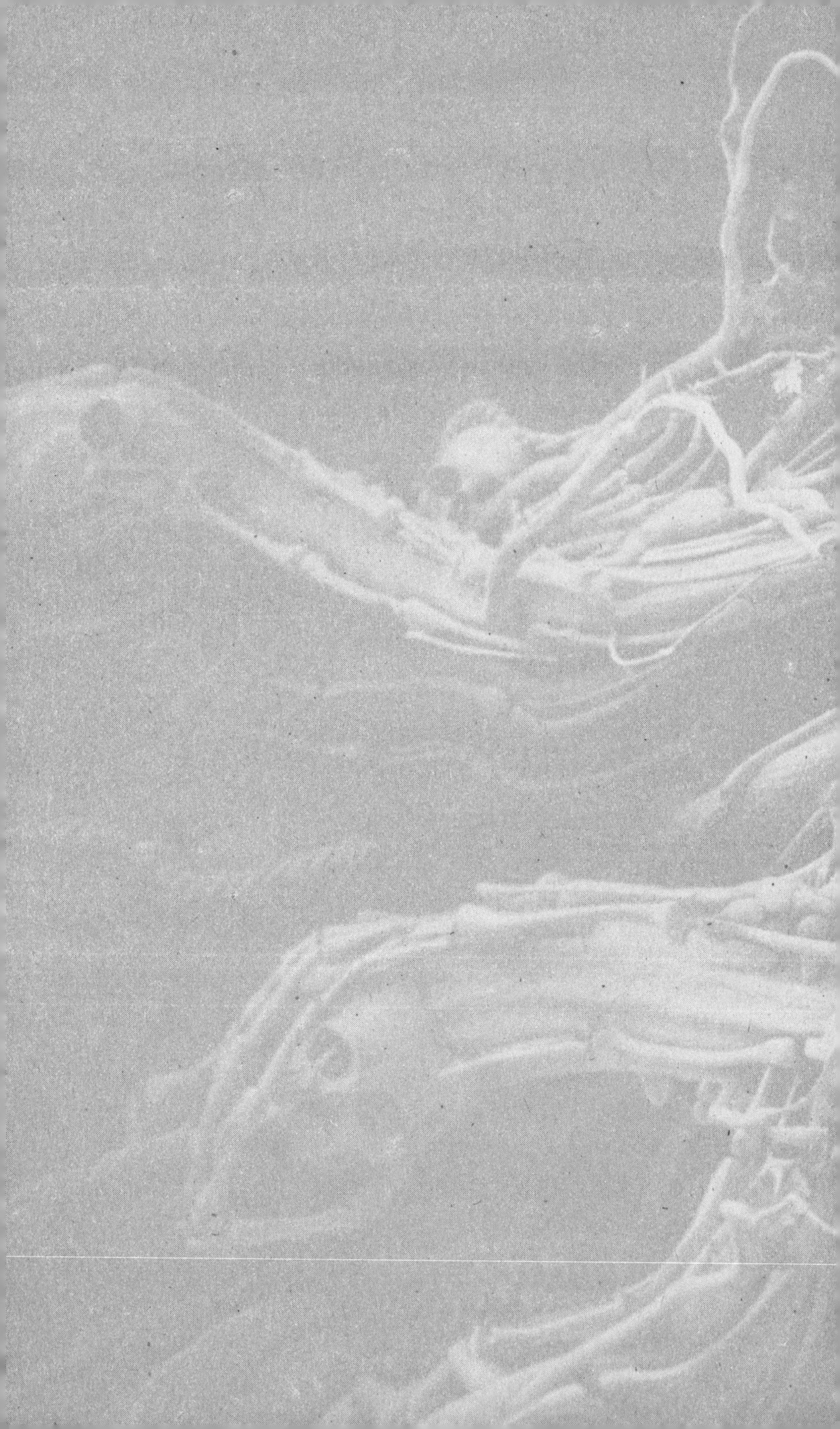

THE UNSEEN WORLD: BOOK TWO

A SLEIGHT OF SHADOWS

KAT HOWARD

LONDON SYDNEY NEW YORK TORONTO NEW DELHI

1230 AVENUE OF THE AMERICAS, NEW YORK, NEW YORK 10020

First Saga Press trade paperback edition June 2024

SAGA PRESS and colophon are trademarks of Simon & Schuster, LLC

Simon & Schuster: Celebrating 100 Years of Publishing in 2024

For information about special discounts for bulk purchases, please contact Simon & Schuster Special Sales at 1-866-506-1949 or business@simonandschuster.com.

The Simon & Schuster Speakers Bureau can bring authors to your live event. For more information or to book an event, contact the Simon & Schuster Speakers Bureau at 1-866-248-3049 or visit our website at www.simonspeakers.com.

Interior design by Erika R. Genova

Manufactured in the United States of America

1 3 5 7 9 10 8 6 4 2

Library of Congress Cataloging-in-Publication Data is available.

ISBN 978-1-5344-2681-8
ISBN 978-1-5344-2682-5 (pbk)
ISBN 978-1-5344-2683-2 (ebook)

To the readers who wanted to know more of Sydney's story.
Thank you for waiting until I got it right.

I'm the phoenix and the ash

–Dessa, "5 out of 6"

A SLEIGHT OF SHADOWS

CHAPTER ONE

The woman sitting at the table cast no shadow.

She should have. The light in the apartment drew grey veils from the coffee cup, empty, on the counter, the chair in which the woman sat, the small white candle in front of her.

It had been just over seven weeks—fifty-three days, exactly—since Sydney had given up her shadow in the final challenge of the Turning. Since she had asked Verenice Tenebrae to cut it from her body so she could sacrifice it to keep magic in the world.

In that time, she had grown accustomed to the lack of her shadow. It had been strange, at first, the absence. The first few days there had been a constant sense that something was missing. The half breath before she put a name, again, to what wasn't there had felt—each time—stretched and strained.

But her shadow wasn't her only loss. It wasn't even the most important one, merely the symbol of what had been given up. When Sydney sacrificed her shadow, she sacrificed her magic. And even now, even now when she no longer reached for a spell in the same way that she used to—the automatic way that blood moved through her veins and breath moved in her lungs—she didn't need to be reminded that that ability was gone. That absence was a constant ache. It lingered in her scars and in her bones, in the places where magic had been cut out of her. The loss was a reminder of what she had been.

Magic had been her entire life. It was her earliest memory, her first, her primary purpose. It was what she had been shaped for. It became the edge against which she honed herself, the means to all her ends. It had been hers—solely hers, not a weapon for the House of Shadows to use as it pleased—for so little time before it was gone.

She wanted it back.

She had a starting point. One remaining scrap. Not enough to do anything that she couldn't more easily accomplish by flipping a switch. Not enough to distinguish her from a mundane person who'd been lucky enough to wander into one of the kinder corners of the Unseen World, and who had enough determination to remain there.

She could still light a candle. She had just enough magic to give her hope.

It was a cruel hope, one as sharp as the knife that had cut away her shadow and her magic. An ache to match the absence. But leaning into the sharp edge of the impossible was what she knew.

Sydney shook off her thoughts and focused on the candle in front of her. A small white tea light in a battered tin, the kind that was sold in bags of one hundred and smelled vaguely of vanilla and plastic. Simple. Basic.

Her first bag was nearly empty. She had others.

Sydney spoke the word that kindled the spell, and the candle lit, just as it always did. Even the first time after the loss of her shadow, and her magic with it. In that flickering moment, she had burned, too. Burned with the hope that she had been wrong, that her magic wasn't gone, that everything would go back to normal. It hadn't. Not that day, and not any of the days since.

An ache throbbed behind her eyes, and the taste of smoke coated her throat—the aftereffects of using magic making themselves known. They came on quicker now, one more reminder that things had changed.

Sydney focused again. Magic required preparation in a way that it never used to. Breathing in, she twisted her left hand, bent two fingers sharply. This was the second spell she tried every day. The spell that would extinguish the candle she had just lit.

Pain like fire licked along the frayed edges where her shadow had been cut away from her body. A phantom blade sliced its way across her bones, tracing over the places where her magic had once been carved out of her.

The candle flickered, dimmed.

Sydney gritted her teeth against the pain and waited, watched. Held her focus. Blood dripped from her nose. The candle guttered.

And went out.

Sydney scrubbed her blood from the kitchen table and threw the extinguished candle in the trash. Once was nothing. Coincidence. A draft in her apartment, an errant exhale. The pain where her shadow had been merely the itch of an amputated limb, the timing coincidence. Nothing more. She couldn't let it be more, not without proof.

She took another candle from the bag, set it on the table.

She breathed in, spreading her awareness throughout her body, searching for anything that felt like magic, for anything that felt like change. For anything different at all. But there was nothing new, nothing beyond what she felt every time she cast this spell: her self, and the absence where her magic had been.

She spoke the word to light the candle.

It flared. A column of fire stretching almost to her ceiling, melting the wax in the tin into immediate nothingness, then extinguishing. The edges of her shadow white hot, as if they were being carved away by a thin knife.

Sydney placed her hands flat on her table, fingers starfished around the burnt-out—consumed—candle. She breathed out.

Her phone rang. One of the few numbers she had promised, always, to answer. "Grace? It's not really a good—"

Grace's voice thin and tight. "Sydney, something weird is happening. I'm in a car outside. You need to come now."

The end of the Turning had seen House Prospero elevated to the head of the Unseen World. Which meant that—as well as the responsibility for House Prospero itself—would have been Sydney's, had she not sacrificed her magic. She had been prepared to die in the course of the Turning, and her fight against the abomination that was the House of Shadows, and so Sydney had named Grace Valentine her heir. For the Unseen World, the loss of magic was equivalent to death.

She had not anticipated the circumstances of Grace's inheritance but remained confident in her choice, especially now that she had seen Grace in her role. She felt more sorrow than she had expected to over the loss of House Prospero. Not for herself so much as for the House, which had genuinely tried, in the short time it had been hers, to be a place of welcome and refuge. But the House loved Grace as well.

She had no regret at all over not being forced to be in charge of the snarl of egos and entitlement that was the Unseen World. If that had been left up to her, she would have undone the entire thing.

She had thought about leaving after the dust of the Turning had settled—getting out of New York, away from the

Unseen World. It might have been better, easier, had she gone away and not looked back. But she hadn't even lived outside the House of Shadows for a full year. Everything, everyone she knew was here. Every time her finger hovered over the button to buy plane tickets, leaving had felt like one loss too many.

And so here she was, sitting in the back of a cab with Grace, on her way to something weird.

Windshield wipers thunked against the glass as tires whirred over rain-slick streets. The car's defrost, the driver had assured them, only worked when the air conditioner was on, as it was now, at full blast. The cold air settled into Sydney's joints, and she wished she had grabbed a warmer coat.

"So when you say weird," she began, suspecting already what the answer would involve. Magic of some sort, doing something that skewed beyond unexpected and into alarming. She wasn't quite sure why that meant she was needed, but Grace wasn't prone to drama, so if she wanted Sydney with her, Sydney would trust that there was a good reason.

"It'll be easier to explain once we're there. I wouldn't have believed it if I hadn't seen it myself." Tension held Grace in rigid lines. She had cast a series of spells as Sydney got in the car—to prevent the driver from overhearing them, to clear a path through traffic. She had tried to redirect the air-conditioning as well, but it really was stubbornly connected to the defrost.

"Nothing good, then." Sydney's hands still ached as if she had been casting far more complicated spells than a simple candle flicker. She curled them into fists to stop the shaking, pressed her fists into her thighs.

"No. Nothing good." They rode the rest of the way in silence.

The scope of the nothing good began to unfold itself as the car stopped at Central Park. The two women raised umbrellas, and Sydney kept pace as Grace walked toward the reservoir. She knew the path. Had walked it again and again at the behest of the House of Shadows, then on her own once she had finally broken free. She had walked this way when she came to destroy the House of Shadows, to render it into rubble and free the sacrifices held inside, and then when she had made the mistake that had led to her own undoing, when she freed Shara from the island that bound her.

She had not come this way since.

They rounded the path, and she saw. "What in the actual fuck." Not a question, a flat statement of disbelief, stark enough to freeze Grace's hand partway through an unveiling spell.

"You can see it?"

"It's not veiled." The House of Shadows, the island it stood on, had been hidden before, magic drawn over it to keep it from mundane sight.

"It is, Syd. The spell's in place."

Had it been anything else, anything other than that island,

full of the bones of the sacrifices who had died in the House of Shadows, their magic carved out of them, that island where now—somehow—walls were once again rising in pieces out of the dirt—Sydney might have found the fact that she could see through the spell interesting, as a data point. She might have paused to wonder what it meant. But as soon as the thought crossed her mind, she knew: "It wants me to see it."

Unable to move or look away, she watched as broken stone slid across barren ground. "How?"

She had left the House of Shadows in ruins. Pulled it apart, unmade it with her magic. Separated stone from stone. She had left it for dead, and somehow it was resurrecting.

"Magic," Grace said. "And I mean that as literally as possible. As far as I can tell, Shadows is rebuilding itself. Not because of outside magic. Because the pieces of the spell that created it are trying to come back together."

"*Magic* wants that place to come back." Bile rose in Sydney's throat along with the words. But even as she spoke, the thought made a kind of sense.

Shadows had always had its own strange kind of agency. It had been capable of changing shape and altering its dimensions on a whim. Magic, especially big, long-running spells like the ones that had animated the House of Shadows had a sort of memory. They *wanted* to continue. That kind of magic meant not just pushing against entropy but turning it inside out and backward, and made order become preferable to chaos.

And magic never particularly cared *how* it was used. Only that it was.

"Can you feel it?" Sydney asked.

When Grace had become the head of the Unseen World, the Houses had mapped themselves onto her body. She could feel their presence, the warm hum of connected magic.

"No, I can't."

"That's good, at least. If anything about this can be said to be good."

"Sydney, I hate asking, but I need you to come out there with me. You know that place better than anyone."

Sydney wanted, very much, to feel as if she could refuse. "I should have sunk that place when I left it."

Grace called a boat from the depths of the lake. This summoning was different from the one Sydney had used to ferry herself back and forth when Shara had compelled her presence, but it was still similar enough to cause her to shudder as she stepped aboard. This was not a journey she had ever thought to make again, even with magic. Without . . . She set her jaw and forced her spine straight. She didn't have the luxury of weakness.

The water was a dull, echoless pewter as Grace and Sydney sailed over it to where the House of Shadows once stood. As they drew closer, Sydney could hear the groan and scrape as its ruins tried to refit themselves. The sound was a nauseating wrongness.

"I hate this place. Everything about it. Even the ground feels haunted," Grace said as they stepped ashore.

"That wouldn't surprise me," Sydney said. "The House of Shadows literally sat on bones. There are bodies all over the island."

Grace froze mid-step, then set her foot down very delicately. "What?"

"All of the sacrifices, all of the magicians who died in Shadows, they're buried beneath the foundations. Bones hold magic—Shara wouldn't have let that go to waste. Service to the House would last until it had extracted every scrap of magic that it could."

"I hadn't thought about that, but of course it makes sense. And is fantastically creepy." Grace looked askance at the ground and then continued walking.

"Did you expect anything different from this place?"

"No, I can't say that I did."

The wind blew hollow, bitter and harsh, scattering dirt and detritus everywhere, reaching beneath the hem of Sydney's jacket, into her sleeves. Shadows' rebuilding didn't look organized, at least not that she could tell. Chunks of ruins heaped together here and there, hulking up out of the ground at random, rather than in straight-lined walls. It didn't look like a House, didn't look like a building. Not yet, anyway. Still. It shouldn't have been happening at all.

"The magic's so sticky and thick that I feel like I'm walking through spiderwebs," Grace said. "Everything clings."

"I can taste it." It clogged Sydney's throat, dry as dust. Arid. "This is different than it was before."

"That's what I thought. But I wasn't sure, and—" Grace swallowed the rest of the sentence.

"And I know Shadows better than anyone." Sydney finished for her. She had lived there almost her entire life and been bound to the place even after she had left. Had been one of two magicians ever to earn her freedom from that binding. Had been the one who had known Shadows well enough to break it.

Now she was broken, and the House of Shadows was unbreaking itself, and that was even more bitter than the magic clogging her throat. That she could sense the magic this intensely felt like another kind of torment—like the House wanting her to. She hadn't lost her ability to sense magic when she lost the ability to cast it, but this, being surrounded like this, felt like a kind of gloating.

The ground shifted under her feet as she walked, as if the reverberation of her steps through the layers of soil and bone disturbed them, as if the bones of the dead were reaching up for her in response. She placed her feet carefully—when Shadows had been whole, when she had been its prisoner, one of its favorite tricks had been to open the floor beneath her and send her plummeting. It had been one of the first ways she had learned to fight Shadows—to pit her will against that of the House and force her way out of where it had dropped her back to some temporarily safer place.

She pushed a loose piece of stone from a broken wall, listened to it crack and rattle as it fell to the ground. Waited for it to crawl its way back to where it had been.

But the stone stayed where it had fallen, and the next scrape of ruin over earth was two different hunks—a broken stair and what might have been a window or doorframe—coming together.

"Have you tried using magic to stop the rebuilding?" Sydney asked. The ground moved beneath her again. Not a tremble so much as a heartbeat. Soft, regular. Flickers of white, like candle flames, sparked at the edges of her vision.

Grace nodded. "It rebuilt as soon as I took it apart. Fast. Almost like it fed on the magic I used."

Sydney swore, low and viciously.

"Agreed," Grace said. "I don't know what to do, Sydney."

"Neither do I."

Grace shivered in the cold. "The rain's getting worse. We should go."

Sydney stared back over the ruins and shook her head. "I should have drowned this place."

But she wondered, as the boat ferried them back to the opposite shore, as she heard the echoing scrape of rock over bone recede behind her, if even that would have been enough.

There is a fountain at the heart of Central Park with a statue of an angel rising from it. Designed by Emma Stebbins and dedicated in 1873, she is called the *Angel of the Waters*. She holds a lily in her hand and was commissioned as a sign of blessing, of healing powers, of an end to the plague of cholera that had ravaged the city.

The statue is very recognizable, the showpiece of the elegant Bethesda Terrace at the heart of Central Park. It is a favorite spot of film crews craving a picturesque location shot and of lovers who wish a romantic setting to exchange promises in. A symbol as resonant as that has its own kind of inherent magic.

In the more recent past, that magical resonance had been taken advantage of, and the *Angel* used as a magical anchor for some of the foulest spells the Unseen World had known. She was made a conduit for the theft of power, a channel for suffering. She had crumbled under the weight of those spells and been repaired only by their end. And so once restored, she was also a symbol of promises made, and promises broken, and power no one should have.

For those who knew how to look. For those who were willing to see. For most people, even for the magicians who should have known differently, she was only a statue.

For a brief time after the statue was made whole again, it seemed as if things might have truly changed. As if the Unseen World might heal and grow into the better thing some hoped it could be. But then, one night not long after the broken ruins of the House of Shadows began to put themselves back together, magic coursed through the statue again. A new magic, but one familiar in its foulness. The spells of the House of Shadows reaching out and attempting to reestablish themselves. Overwhelmed, the lily cracked and fell from the hand of the *Angel*. That offering of hope, of peace, of continued growth and new life, shattered.

That shattering was not the only piece of strangeness to occur that night. Even as the wind scattered bits of the broken statue, a group of trees stretched and rose from the earth throughout Central Park. They unfurled into full growth almost as soon as they broke free from the soil. At the heart of each tree was a bone. A human bone. A piece of who those trees had once been.

Whisperings rose with them—the trees speaking their memories. Memories of loneliness, abandonment. Of a house made of shadows, and magic sharp as knives. Of pain, and then of death. It was a heartbreaking, haunting sound. The mournful voices of the trees were an ache to listen to, a veil of grief draped over skin. They permeated the park, inescapable.

Magic clouded the air like fog. Something was beginning.

CHAPTER TWO

The great Houses of the Unseen World were crumbling.

It is usually nothing of consequence to find that an old house—and these Houses were old, some of the oldest things built in this relative upstart of a city—has cracked its foundation, requires a new roof, or has developed recalcitrant plumbing. Such things happen even when Houses are spelled and reinforced with magic. Magic, like wallpaper, occasionally curls at its edges.

But these cracks and breaks, these flaws in the Houses were not fixable. The magicians who held them tried. But any repairs made by mundane labor undid themselves by the next dawn. Any attempt at repair by magic made the damage worse, as if magic itself was the rot in the walls, as if feeding that rot increased it.

Even though they could all see it happening, not just in their own Houses but in others, no one spoke of it at first. The Houses, after all, were intimately connected to those who held them. To hold a House in the Unseen World required establishing a worthiness to belong, meant surviving the Turning, that tournament of magic that pitted magician against magician, even to the death. It meant binding a physical house as part of the self, a tangible symbol of that survival, that strength, that worth.

The strength of the magician was reflected in the strength of the House. Houses that crumbled meant a weakness in magic, meant a weak, crumbling magician, and the Unseen World was not the sort of place that tolerated weakness.

But whispers crept like vines between houses, confirming that this breaking, this rot, this malfunctioning magic was spreading. Old spells long cast re-emerged in bits and pieces, in kitchens and closets, magic flickering in and out of existence like hauntings. Grand illusions that had been cast by House champions during Turnings manifested in spare bedrooms and basements. Fragments of spells slid downstairs in loops, the magic repeating itself like a skipping record.

The Unseen World's magic leaked from its roofs, moldered its floorboards, cracked its foundations. The breaking spells smelled like charnel houses, like mausoleums, like dirt and darkness and bone. The Houses, even the most spacious, felt claustrophobic, like their walls had grown too close. They felt crowded, even when empty, as if they were peopled by watching ghosts.

The whispers of the magicians grew louder, grew into low-voiced conversations, turned into narrowed eyes that searched for causes and searched more diligently for blame.

The latter was easy enough to place.

There was one House that remained unaffected: House Prospero. Alone of all the great Houses of the Unseen World, it showed no alteration, no visible change in its magic, and wasn't that odd, when all of magic had been so recently changed by someone who had held that House.

When Sydney cut off the Unseen World's connection to the House of Shadows, she had changed magic. She had taken away its ease from all of them. Magic *hurt* now.

Perhaps what hurt the magician hurt the House.

Everyone felt very publicly virtuous about loudly turning their backs on the former House of Shadows, about visibly washing their hands clean of its tainted magic. But some people also began, privately, to wonder if perhaps things hadn't been better before, when magic was painless, and their Houses stood strong. They considered, quietly, whether there might be a way to go back.

Dahlia Morgan, petite, thin, precise, dressed in tailored cream silk that stains would be afraid to land on, watched as the dirt settled around the sunflowers she had planted for her sister Rose. They were replacements. She had awoken the day before to discover that half the plants in her yard had turned to stone overnight. Most of them she would leave until the issues with magic sorted themselves out, but she didn't want Rose to be without flowers.

Rose had loved sunflowers, had joked that the reason was

that the name was one of the few too ridiculous for their parents to use to name one of them—all of the Morgan girls had floral names.

They had planted roses on her grave, but here, at House Morgan, Dahlia had given her sister sunflowers.

Dahlia had thought she would feel better after seeing Grey Prospero—the man who had murdered Rose for her magic—die in the Turning. But in the end, it hadn't been enough. What she wanted was Rose back, and there was no magic in the world that could do that. Plus, the circumstances of the challenge—the conjured images of Rose and the other women, the death that had echoed theirs—had felt too much. Too close to turning suffering into theater. She hadn't felt better; she had only felt raw all over again.

The Turning. The end of it had ruined everything. One person's decision, and the entire Unseen World was changed. Dahlia wiped away the blood that dripped from her nose, the aftereffect of using magic to plant the sunflowers.

The Unseen World was changed, and not for the better. Magic required sacrifice, that was true, but the House of Shadows had ensured that sacrifice was a collective one. Each House contributed so each House received benefits. Without that order, that connection, everything was falling apart.

It was a waste. Dahlia looked over her yard again, noting what was stone and what was blooming. Letting the Unseen World falter and weaken like this, especially when that could be prevented, was a waste of what had built it. She brushed her hand against the bright, gold petals of the sunflower. She hated waste.

Catriona Don is at the door.

House Morgan's voice had gone staticked and glitchy, the scratch of a record needle after the music had run out. Dahlia stifled a wince, as she did every time the House spoke these days. It wasn't the House's fault.

The altered voice was only one of the changes plaguing House Morgan. Aside from half of the yard recently being rendered into statuary, there were cracks in the walls from where the foundation had shifted. Feathers, soft white down, fell from the cracks constantly. A bathroom faucet dripped salt water, and there was no way to turn it off. Every morning, the front hall floor was covered with dead leaves, as if autumn had blown in overnight.

It was June.

Another set of leaves, oak, the faded sepia of old photography, appeared in the wake of the door as she opened it.

"You have leaves?" Catriona asked as she stepped over the threshold. "We have frogs."

"Frogs?" Dahlia repeated.

"Like some sort of biblical plague, yes. It's vulgar. This entire thing is, really, the poor Houses, our magic not working properly, and painful when it does. Ridiculous."

Without waiting for Dahlia, Catriona made her way to the kitchen. "Ask the House for a green smoothie for me, would you? I came straight from the gym."

She did not, Dahlia thought, with the exception of the bright pink athleisure clinging to her tall, muscular frame, particularly look like she had come from the gym. Her expensively blond hair looked professionally blown out, her golden skin tastefully made up and flawless. Catriona did not look like someone who did anything so human as sweat.

Dahlia asked for a mug of her favorite jasmine green tea to accompany Catriona's smoothie, then hissed as the magical backlash spiked pain just behind her eyes.

"Like I said, ridiculous. Something needs to be done. How well do you know Grace Valentine?" Catriona tapped long, manicured nails the same frothed green as her smoothie against the glass.

"Only slightly." Dahlia sipped at her tea, settling herself. "But she's very tight with Sydney and that contingent, so I doubt she's likely to be sympathetic."

Catriona's lip curled in distaste. "Lesser Houses and outsiders, all of them. No one who has a clue about how things are actually supposed to run. Still, you would have thought one of them might have figured out by now that things were fucked up, and that there was an easy fix."

Dahlia sipped her tea, then shuddered and set it aside. It had arrived cold and bitter, and fixing it magically was not at all worth the consequences. "How easy would it be, do you think?"

The taller woman's gaze sharpened. "Depends on what's left, probably. Sydney cut off the spell, but if there are remnants of it? Or if the House of Shadows itself is left? I wasn't Head of House the last time House Don made its sacrifice, but you've been there, right?"

"Yes. I know the spells to get there, if any of them are still necessary." They might not be, depending on the state of the magic and the House.

"It's not the only thing that matters, of course, but having the House would be a good start." A floorboard sprang loose under Catriona's bag, knocking it over and sending her water bottle rolling. The sulfuric stench of rotten eggs emerged from beneath the loose floorboard.

Catriona swore as she crouched to gather her things. "Something needs to be done now, before this gets any worse."

"I'll go to the island." Dahlia's face was twisted with disgust, and she held her hand over her mouth and nose to block the smell. "You see who else might be willing to support a return to sanity."

"Done." The two women fled the room.

House Merlin was one of the thirteen founding Houses of the Unseen World. It had been in continuous existence ever since. It had proved its strength in Turning after Turning, never being cast out or unmade.

It had been powerful once, both in the magicians who were born or brought into it, and in its physical incarnation: a grand and intimidating mansion, responsive to the wants of its holder. But like all once-grand things, eventually it began to wear and show its age. Its magicians became less capable. What power they did have expressed itself politically, in the machinations of governing the Unseen World, rather than magically. This seemed like the turn of Fortune's Wheel—some Houses rose, others fell, and things would spin again. Not ideal for those on the falling arc, but no cause for concern, so long as one remained on the wheel in anticipation of the next rise to power. House Merlin had been great before and surely would be great again. And then the House passed to Miles Merlin.

Miles had never been a particularly strong magician, and what magic he had slipped through his fingers like sand, flowing faster and faster the harder he tried to hold on to it. After a few years under his tenure, House Merlin could have been anyone's—it was no longer bound to him, it held no inherent magic, and the building had become so mundane that Miles filled it with an excess of technology in an attempt to hide what was lacking, both in the House and in himself. Eventually, for all his increasingly panicked grasping, Miles' own magic completely disappeared.

The consequences to the Unseen World from his attempt to hide this were tremendous.

But now Miles was gone, cast out from the Unseen World, and House Merlin belonged to Miles' youngest child, Lara. She had never expected to hold the House, had always assumed it would go to her older brother, Ian, and so had never spent time imagining how it would be if she did. Even if she had, no amount of imagining would have prepared her for the current situation. Because of her father's lack of care, there was no thread of magic connecting her to the place. She had no idea how to create one. She wondered, idly, if she should move. Start over, find a place that felt like hers. The point of holding a House was maintaining that connection between person, place, and magic. It was meant to be a relationship. There was nothing like that for her in the House as it was.

The current House wasn't even the sort of place she would have chosen for herself. Not just because of Miles' penchant for stark white and chrome, for a sterile sort of decorating that would have fit better in a lab. It was that the very air of the place seemed cold, hostile. Bereft of any feeling of welcome or comfort.

It hadn't always been that way. House Merlin had been a comfort to her when she was younger, had been a refuge from Miles' moods. When that stopped, when the House seemed to ignore her, she had been heartbroken. She had thought the House no longer liked her. She realized now that it simply hadn't had enough magic to interact with anyone other than its Head.

She could move. It would be unusual for an established

House to change its physical residence, but it had been done. There were precedents. And a clean slate might be preferable—better to mark a difference between who she was and what she wanted her House to be and what House Merlin recently had been. Miles' deceptions, the connections to the House of Shadows. Everything she wished had never happened. Everything that still made her stomach clench in mortification over her connection to it.

Still. The House was hers now, and she had loved it once. She owed that remembered love the effort to restore it, to make it whole again, to bring it back to being a place of warmth and sanctuary. At the very least, she could make it feel like someplace she actually wanted to live.

She had started with her bedroom, using magic to paint the walls and ceiling the sherbet-toned pinks and oranges of a sunset. The spell had been difficult at first—like running without warming up—but had grown easier as it progressed. Once she had made the change, the House felt just a little friendlier, a little more hers. It was a good start, and, encouraged, she threw herself into the project.

"What are you doing?" Ian asked.

Lara said a quick spell so that the paint roller would ease itself back into the tray, rather than drop from where it worked, and reminded herself that she needed to set up a doorbell spell. She didn't mind that Ian had let himself in, but without magic in the House, anyone could do the same.

Locks were so ineffective against magicians that most Houses—House Merlin included—didn't have physical ones at all, relying solely on magic to control access. If Miles had installed one, it would have been a remarkable enough change to cause gossip. Now it was simply one more thing that needed dealing with.

An entire wall of the living room was now a bright, electric blue. Streaks and splatters of the paint decorated Lara's hands. "Making some changes."

Ian spun slowly, taking in the room. "I like it. It looks like you."

"It makes me happy." She shoved her hair back, leaving blue splotches in the fuchsia strands. "I'm hoping it will make the House happy, too."

"It already feels better than it did when Miles was here," Ian said. "More welcoming. Less cold."

"I just don't want it to feel like it's still his." Lara's mouth twisted.

"With you in charge? And looking like this? Not a chance."

"Do you think he'll come back?" Lara asked. "That we'll ever see him again?"

"No," Ian said. "There's no profit in it for him, nothing he could game to be who he thought he deserved to be. Not anymore."

She nodded. "That's what I think, too." Miles hadn't reached out to her at all after she had helped expose his deception and lack of magic. He had simply left. Emails bounced; no phone calls went through. She had not tried anything more than that to find him.

"Is there something I can help with while I'm here?" Ian asked.

"Well, I was hoping you might want to visit more now. So if you wanted to pick a guest room, paint it however you like, even if that means boring white walls."

He laughed. "Maybe I'll go crazy, splash out into beige or paint the trim navy. Thanks, Lara."

Verenice's house was on the outside of the city, away from the Unseen World. In the summer, it was a lushness of flowers. They filled her window boxes, sat in containers on her stoop, wound delicately up a trellis and wall in an explosion of color and scent.

Sydney had grown to love spending time there. There was the peace and quiet pleasure of sitting in the garden. But beyond that, she had learned that she loved the feeling of dirt beneath her fingers as she helped Verenice plant. Her hands ached less from the loss of her magic when she was using them to coax green and life out of the earth. She felt almost like herself again when she was gardening.

They worked half the morning before Sydney broke the spell of the place.

"Shadows is *growing* back?" Verenice said. She had withdrawn into herself as Sydney spoke, her own barriers rising against the horrors of Shadows, against the memories of her imprisonment and torture there.

"That's the best way I can describe it. It's unorganized and chaotic, but also inexorable. It started this on its own. I'd say it was like weeds in a garden, but that's too slight for what I saw." Sydney patted dirt into place and slid the container, now full of sunset-colored marigolds, toward Verenice.

Verenice sighed out a long breath as she reached for the flowers. "I wish that I were more surprised."

"That's how I feel, too, now that I'm past the initial shock. It feels almost as if it was made to come back." The truth of the words was a slime in her throat. "Like there was some sort of fail-safe in the spell. I should have thought further, should have realized no place like that could ever just be stopped. The Unseen World had too much riding on its continued existence."

Verenice shook her head. "You can't blame yourself for what you didn't know."

"Can't I?" Her mouth twisted bitterly. "It only took eleven days after I severed the spell for the first person to contact Grace about bringing it back. Even if I didn't know, I should have seen."

"Sydney."

"What I can see, now, is every single thing I should have done differently, all of the choices that I should have made. Then I wonder: If magic itself really is the thing that brought

Shadows back, would it have undone all of those other choices anyway?"

"The return of Shadows might not be the only strange thing happening with magic, from what I've heard," Verenice said.

"The bone trees?" Sydney asked, allowing the shift in the subject. "They're heartbreaking. Haunting. Have you visited them yet?"

"I have." Verenice's hands stilled. "I recognized too many voices. But I was actually thinking of the Houses. Shadows, for all that it was a horror of one, was a House of the Unseen World. I wonder if what is happening to the others is connected to it."

"Oh?" Sydney paused in her work as well. Even though Verenice lived apart from the Unseen World, she kept diligent track of its doings.

"Something has gone wrong with nearly all of them. Prospero seems to be the only one that's unaffected. The magic of the Houses has gone strange, for lack of a better word. They are decaying, wearing down, but all at once. And there have been outbursts of magic as well—spells that no one cast and no one can halt."

"So magic is upset about something. Nice that it waited until now to express that." Sydney's words razor-edged, her movements forceful as she planted the next set of flowers.

"I don't pretend to understand it, either, Sydney."

"You're right that it's oddly similar—especially the spells casting on their own," Sydney thought out loud. "Are the

Houses falling down because Shadows is rebuilding, or is magic just a mess generally? Does magic even see the idea of mess? Because I kind of suspect not, all things considered.

"And why do I even care so much what the actual cause is when it's not like there's even one useful fucking thing I can do about it."

Snap.

The sharp scent of broken chlorophyll and a stickiness on her fingers. A bright orange marigold tumbled to the ground, a miniature sun falling from the sky.

"Verenice, I'm sorry." Sydney patted the dirt around the broken plant, as if apologizing to it as well.

"Oh my dear, so am I." Their eyes met.

Verenice stood. "I think perhaps that's enough for today. Will you help me put away the containers?"

"Of course." Sydney patted the dirt once more, then stood up.

A green shoot unfurled from the broken plant. It stretched into a leaf, then budded and bloomed. By the time the container had been placed with the others, there was no longer a trace of where the flower had been broken.

Sydney had never learned to sleep well or deeply. The House of Shadows had not been, by its nature, a place conducive to rest even when it wasn't purposefully keeping her restless and stressed. After she had left it, her own vigilance meant she was often insomniac and wakeful.

Ever since she had seen the pieces of Shadows rising from the earth, when she did sleep, it was with the echo of rocks scraping over bone in her head. The noise was a constant background, a kind of aural haunting. It didn't go quiet until she woke, and then the silence would be an overloud, oppressive pause, her body full of the seasick anticipation that the worst was still waiting to happen.

It had woken her again.

She sat back against her headboard, knees pulled up, fingers idly shifting through the shapes of spells. Her apartment was too quiet, and still the silence too loud. The House of Shadows, a pair of claws sunk in the base of her skull.

She'd lived with the same sensation before, when she was still bound to Shadows, when the House could summon her, could force her to return at its whim. But it seemed weightier now. Maybe that was simply because she'd gotten used to its absence. Or maybe it was the absence of her magic that altered things. Maybe she had less strength to carry the burden.

Shivering, she pulled up another blanket from the pile at the foot of her bed. Here, alone in the dark, there was no other choice but to admit that was what frightened her. That this time, she was lacking. That this time, she wouldn't be enough, not even close to enough to stand against the House of Shadows and the magic that was rebuilding it.

That there was nothing more left of her than the flickering light of a candle.

She reached inside herself, searching. Crackles of raw nerves traced their way across her bones, sparking though the lines that had been carved there. Her hands ached, as though she had spent the night casting spells.

There was a whited-out hollowness where her shadow should have been.

There was a story she knew a piece of, a boy who had lost his shadow through some misadventure, and a girl, carefully sewing it back on for him, the needle passing through flesh and bone. Sydney wished things were that easy, that all she needed to do was find her shadow, and then the right needle and thread to sew it on with. Was the needle made of bone? The thread of sinew? Or were they ordinary objects, the only magic needed desire and belief? Her thoughts clung to the details of an impossible solution, puzzling out the specifics as if they might someday be applicable. But her shadow wasn't lost. It was gone. Severed. Sacrificed.

It hadn't been a clean cut, when Verenice had sliced her shadow from her. There were still raw edges, frayed ends. She had thought, once, that those might be her way back to magic—that perhaps her shadow might regrow, or she might be able to find other scraps of shadows to weave into them. She had considered every possible solution, and some impossible ones besides. None had worked.

Magic cared about will, about intent. Sydney had meant for the loss of her shadow to be a sacrifice of magic, and so that was what it was. If she had any magic left to her, it wouldn't be found in those remnant shreds. She looked at her hands again, flexing her fingers against the ache that lingered in her bones.

Then she pushed her blankets aside and got out of bed.

As she had every day since Sydney had told her of the House of Shadows' return, Verenice walked out onto her porch in the evening. The fragrance of her garden filled the air around her: the bright spice of the marigolds, the heady honey of the roses, the ripe lushness of leaf and stem and green. Their shadows stretched long and long as the sun sank, and that, too, was what she needed.

The spot she sat in to work changed slightly every time, shifting with the sun. Verenice watched her shadow roll out before her, a black velvet train. She picked up an edge of it, drew in a breath, and set her teeth. Then began, Penelope-like, to unweave.

One thread of her shadow, pulled delicately loose, and then carefully, carefully separated from the rest. It felt like nails slicing inside her skin, both raw and wrong.

The first time she had unwoven a thread from her shadow, she had vomited from the pain. It hadn't become any less viscerally upsetting, but she was better able to brace herself now.

The separated thread clung, sticky, to her fingers. She kept a smooth tension in it, breathing deep and slow to keep her hands steady. It was as thin as embroidery floss, and as long as the setting sun would allow her.

She removed only one thread from her shadow at a time. The effects were unendurable otherwise, both during and after.

Once she had that long, thin thread, Verenice passed its entirety through her fingers again. As she did, she whispered the harsh words of a spell that scoured from it everything that was not magic. Cast-off motes shimmered briefly in the air, releasing a warm, campfire scent, before sparking and falling to the ground like dust.

Then Verenice spoke another word, this one sharp, a shattering. Her breath frosted in her mouth. She held the thread of shadow over the still surface of a mirror and then unwound it, the thread sinking into the glass like smoke as she did. After the last bit of shadow slipped through the mirror, Verenice passed her hand over it, closing the spell, locking this thread away with the others she had collected.

Only then did she close her eyes, allow her face and hands to fall into the lines of pain and exhaustion caused by her work. She sat with the sensations, allowing them to stretch to fill every cell, and then, slowly, to recede.

It took more time now, that return to normal. A little longer each day, as she thinned her own shadow. The alteration she was making was not the sort of thing that healed or grew back.

She had known, when Sydney handed her the knife, when she had trusted Verenice to use it, that shadows didn't grow back. She should have refused, should have insisted on another way. Should have done anything but what she did. She would never forgive herself.

This was her chosen amends.

CHAPTER THREE

In Central Park, the bone trees were speaking.

Each tree told its own story, each in its own voice, the sound of who the tree had been in life. Some simply wept, sorrow given root and growth. Others spoke their names over and over, as if that one thing was all they had left to cling to. Some spoke longer—bits and pieces of lives, and of deaths. They spoke even when no one was there to listen, like the telling itself was the key to a ritual. Their voices filled the park like fog, haunting everyone who passed within its bounds.

At the center of each tree, set in notches and hollows like the relics of saints, were bones. Rib cages, spines. Hands, with their delicate finger bones that fell like leaves. The flowers that bloomed from the trees were also made of bone, petal-thin slivers that smelled like dust and time when their fragrance was caught on the wind. The lost and forgotten dead, transmuted into new shapes and trying desperately to be remembered.

Even mundane passersby were affected. They couldn't hear the trees, not quite, nor see them exactly as they were, but they could feel the effects of their presence. They pulled on sweaters, hunched their shoulders against air that was too cold even in the warmth of the summer sun. Felt sorrow drag their steps and tears well from seemingly nowhere. They hurried through the park or changed routes to avoid it.

Sydney watched as a dog walker struggled to comfort a puppy howling at the base of one of the trees. "Poor thing."

"It's awful. All of this." Madison's face was streaked with tears.

"I recognize some of the voices. Verenice did, too. As far as I can tell, each of the trees is a magician who died in the House of Shadows." Sydney shook her head. "I'm not sure what's worse—the fact that I recognize some of them, or the fact that I'm sure that there are others who were there with me that I don't. Ones the House killed quickly, or kept separated, or just that there were so very many that I don't remember all the voices."

"Syd—"

"Or maybe what's worse is that these are the closest thing to graves—to memorials—they have. That the rest of what is left of them is heaped somewhere out on that island. And that Shadows is using their magic, whatever remains of it, still. Again."

Fragments of bone fell through the air, spinning like snow. They had more weight than snow when they landed, sounding almost like the gentle percussion of rain when hitting the ground.

"I think that what's happening here and what's happening

there are somehow connected. Like Shadows waking up woke all of its ghosts, too," Sydney said.

"Has anything changed for you?"

A quick shake of her head. "No, it hasn't." An extinguished candle, sometimes, maybe, was not reawoken magic.

"Ian still being weird about it?"

"He is. He coddles me, like he's afraid I'm going to break any minute. He doesn't get that I am broken, that I am trying to fix myself. I want to visit the archives."

"Well, that's a change of subject." The archives were a magically hidden floor at Wellington & Ketchum, the law firm where Madison was a partner. All their non-mundane records were stored there. It was not a usual sort of storage area, nor one with a traditional filing system.

"It's not, really. Any information I might need about any of this—Shadows, the Houses, any magicians who had their magic restored after having it stripped—if it exists, it will be in there. I need to do something."

"And research is something you can do. I get that. I'll have Harper take you up. They like her."

"They have preferences? Never mind. They're old magic. Of course they do. I'll call your secretary to set it up. Thanks, Madison."

Laurent Beauchamps, Head of the most recently established House of the Unseen World, picked up his tablet and swiped through into his email. After the Turning had ended, after he had earned a place in the hierarchy of the Unseen World, it had been made clear to him that he needed to establish a House and that he needed to do so sooner rather than later. A physical building that would be bound to him by various magical means that no one had quite fully explained yet. He could buy, but there would be an expectation of significant renovation connected to that aforementioned magical binding. New construction would be better.

His inbox was crowded, mostly with messages from architectural firms that had the Unseen World connections to know about and be able to handle the magical requirements of such a house. Some had blueprints attached, and all came with invitations to discuss things further over lunch or drinks. Realtors sent listings with similar offers to follow up at his convenience. It had been years since a new House had been founded in the Unseen World, and everyone was very eager to make sure Laurent got exactly what he wanted, or at least what they thought he should have.

The enthusiasm of a large number of people he'd never met aside, nothing so far was what he was looking for. "I feel like Henry VIII picking out his next castle," he muttered as he scrolled through pictures of various buildings, all of which seemed designed either to intimidate or to showcase excess. In some cases, there was an attempt at both. Nothing looked even remotely appealing. "Would you like a moat to go with your drawbridge, sir, to keep the rabble out? Perhaps some spikes just waiting for the heads of your enemies? You can pay for it with Bitcoin."

The offerings were so bad they were laughable.

Laurent didn't want a House so he could keep people out. He wanted a House that would welcome them in. And not just the people who were already part of the Unseen World, but the people like he had been—the outsiders.

His parents had been high school teachers, not tenth-generation magicians. He'd only known magic as sleight of hand and card tricks, maybe a television special where a car disappeared. But his own magical ability was strongest around luck, which had helped him find his way to the Unseen World. Once he had refined it, it allowed him to make the kind of money that brought him to the level of the established Houses, and had let him hire Sydney to compete as his champion in the Turning. Her performance meant that now he was an established House. Which was a weird thing to be, when House Beauchamps had exactly one member: him.

He pushed back in his chair and rolled the stiffness from his neck. Maybe that was the issue. Maybe he needed to find the people before he decided what sort of House they belonged in. Maybe he needed to let those other magicians—people who barely knew that magic existed or what it could do—know that they had, if not a home, then at least a place to belong.

He clicked open a new file on his tablet and began putting together a spell.

Mia Rodriguez finished the last of her AP Chem homework, tipped back in her chair, and rolled her head in circles. She loved the lab work, but balancing equations got eye-crossing after the twentieth problem in the set. And she still had calc to deal with before she could crash.

Goats. Videos of baby goats would help. Especially the adorable ones that fainted when they were startled. She always felt sort of guilty about laughing at them, but not so much that she didn't have an entire playlist saved. She grabbed her phone and swiped through screens.

An email notification popped up, which was interesting, as she didn't have her email notifications on push. The email wasn't from a sender she knew, though it wasn't from an obvious scammer, either. More interestingly, it had gotten through the special filters she'd set up to keep unwanted trash from corrupting her inbox.

Most interesting, it shimmered. Like someone had dusted highlighter over the letters on the screen. Looking at it, she *wanted* to click. Not like a compulsion, but just a powerful sense of curiosity and a feeling that there was something she wanted to see inside the message.

She hesitated for a moment, her finger hovering over the screen, then opened the email.

It was an invitation. To learn magic.

That's right. Magic. I know how that sounds, but keep

reading. If you're anything like I was, you've noticed things happening and wondered exactly how they did. Maybe you've felt a little weird, or even like you might be crazy. You're not crazy. And you're not alone.

Magic is real, and if you want, I'll help you learn to use yours, and help you find a community of other people with similar gifts.

By the way, don't worry that this was sent to you in error. No non-magical person would see this email, so if you're reading it, you're in.

Magic. Mia could, sometimes, make things move. Not just by thinking about them—she didn't have that sort of control. But when she was really stressed or upset, books would tip off shelves, trash cans fall over, and then there was that time in second grade when Brent Williams' soda upended itself over his head because he wouldn't stop yanking on her hair. Literally picked itself up off the lunch table and poured from above him.

She grinned at the memory. That had been kind of great. Even if she did have to miss recess for a week.

Mia made excuses. Blamed clumsiness. Said she didn't know why things like that happened around her, which had the benefit of being true, even if the adults involved didn't necessarily believe her. Even in second grade, she knew that nothing good would happen if she told people she could move things with her mind.

And then there was the time it didn't work.

It was October of her freshman year of high school, and she'd had the same lunch as Micaela, her sister, who was a junior. Micaela had been halfway across the cafeteria, smiling about whatever she was going to tell Mia, when the shooting started.

Mia had tried so hard to do something, anything—move the gun, the bullets, the chairs and tables—that she had burst blood vessels in her nose and ears. She was so covered in blood that the first responders initially thought she'd been shot.

She hadn't. Micaela had. She was dead before anyone could get to her.

But maybe, maybe if Mia had known how to use this whatever it was she had, this maybe-magic, she would have been able to do something.

Maybe if she learned how to use magic, she'd finally feel safe again.

She checked the listed address. It was a school, a fancy-looking place, brick walls and wrought-iron gates. The Agrippa Academy. There was a date and a time, and a set of instructions to find the classroom. Some of the instructions were ways to get past spells that kept non-magical people from finding their way into the school, and honestly, it would be worth going just to see if she could do those.

Mia hit reply: *I'm in.*

Again and again Sydney's thoughts turned to the bone trees. They didn't have the weight of the awful presence of Shadows, didn't carry the flare of anxiety that arose when she thought of the slowness of her progress with magic. Rather, they lingered, their roots sunk into her brain.

She felt their voices as a kind of restlessness beneath her skin—a restlessness that quieted in their presence. So she went back, and back again, to walk among them and to listen. As if maybe, if she heard their stories often enough, the trees would find peace. If they could, maybe she might.

Laurent had come with her this morning and had been so silent as they walked that she started in surprise when his voice cut through the words of the trees.

"Were there funerals?"

Sydney blinked. "For the Shadows? No. Shara would never have wasted time and energy like that. We were things to be used up and thrown away, nothing more."

"Okay, that is also horrible, but I meant during the Turning. Or after, I guess. I wouldn't have gone to Grey's after learning what he did, but people died, and I never heard anything about funerals. Or memorial services, or anything. For anyone. So I'm wondering if this is something that happened and I wasn't told about it because there wasn't House Beauchamps yet, or if it just never happened."

"Seventeen. Seventeen people, including Grey, died in the course of the Turning. Every established House lost at least one member. Some of the candidate Houses died before they had a chance to be recognized." She had killed more than one of those people herself. She had killed more people than anyone else who had also survived this Turning.

"That is . . . a lot. More than I'd realized." He shook his head as if to clear it. "So what happened?"

"Funerals for those who fall during the Turning are meant to be quiet affairs. Too much fuss would suggest that there is something to fuss about, not just Fortune's Wheel turning and each House's fortunes rising or falling with it." The trees seemed quieter now, the rustle of their leaves and the shiver of their bone blossoms louder than their speech. "And after all, what's left of their magic belongs to everyone now, just like it would have if those magicians had been given to Shadows as sacrifices, so what loss is there, really?"

"Seriously? That's it?"

"If you're a good, proper member of the Unseen World."

They came to a bench. Laurent sat, slumped. "There should have been something more. There should *be* something more. A memorial. Or, I don't know. Something."

"I'm sure there is, somewhere. A tasteful plaque, a list of names no one has to read or see because there's a spell that keeps the dust off. Just enough that they can tell themselves that they've done something, but not enough to make anyone refuse to play the game when it starts the next time."

"Game." Laurent's voice was quiet. "I wish I could disagree." A pause. "And then what about the names that aren't on the plaque? You say you're fine, Syd, but are you? Are you really? You *killed* people for me so that I could establish this House. You could have been killed yourself. And none of that registered to me when the Turning started, not really. Because it was a game to me then. One that I wanted to play, and one that I knew a lot of money would let me win. I hired you, and I asked you to kill for me, and I didn't even think about it beyond winning or losing.

"You're my friend, and I've never even thought to ask you how you've been getting through all of this. This after. Of what I asked you to do." That last sentence half-swallowed, as if even speaking it was too much.

"I killed people to bring down Shadows," Sydney said. "Working for you during the Turning was an opportunity that I took in order to do that. I made my choice. I'd make the same one again."

"Not quite what I asked."

"I know," she said. "I know."

CHAPTER FOUR

Mia couldn't decide if the Agrippa Academy wanted to be noticed or not. With its old bricks and older trees, wrought-iron gate that led to cobblestone paths through perfectly manicured green, it was one of those places that pretended it was subtle when really every angle of it screamed *money*. No one built places like that unless they wanted people to notice them and be impressed and envious.

Except. She had walked by this address hundreds of times and never seen what was definitely an unmissable building. She only saw it now because she knew it was there. So maybe there was some flavor of subtlety at work after all. Maybe what they cared about wasn't whether they were noticed but rather who noticed them.

She put her hand on the locked gate, her stomach churning in a fizz of anticipation and nerves, and spoke the phrase that had been emailed to her.

A scent like a just-extinguished match rose in the air, the afterthought of smoke. The lock shivered and released with a click. The gate swung open.

Magic. She had just—on purpose—done actual magic. Mia grinned. "Cool."

The noise of the city fell away as she stepped through the gate, as if someone had placed a soundproof dome over the academy grounds. The air smelled so fresh and so free of the normal smells of exhaust and concrete that she looked over her shoulder to make sure that the street was still there, that she hadn't stepped into some kind of pocket universe or alternate dimension. But the city was there, and she was here, surrounded by magic.

The email said that the class would be held after hours, so the rooms they needed would be free. As she walked through an empty campus, Mia wished she had come by earlier—she wanted to see what the students here were like, the ones who had known about magic their entire lives. To get an idea of what it might have been like growing up and having something so strange simply be normal. Did they use magic to cook meals and make their beds, or was it something saved for special occasions? Did they know how to fly, or to turn themselves invisible? Could they cure cancer, or keep people from dying?

Was she going to be able to do those things?

As she walked into the main building, Mia rechecked the emailed instructions. She closed her eyes, spun three times counterclockwise, and then stomped her left foot. Partway down the hall, a door opened.

Just like magic.

The room was a normal classroom, if you defined normal as what you'd see in a movie about how a mildly quirky English teacher changed the narrow thinking and lives of her prep school students before some angry parent got her fired precisely because she'd taught their child to think. There were six other people already in there, mostly around Mia's age, their attention half on the door and half on phone screens. No one walking past would have guessed that it was a bunch of maybe-magicians waiting to take their first magic class. Mia slid into a desk in the center, one seat behind the front row. No one sat in the front row.

She had just gotten settled when a plate of brownies flew through the door, across the room, and settled itself neatly in the center of an empty desk.

"Traditionally, the first spell magicians in the Unseen World are taught is lighting a candle. But since we live in a world where we turn on our lights with electricity, I thought we'd start with something a bit more fun: levitation." A tall Black man, about thirty, followed the brownies into the room. "I'm Laurent Beauchamps. Glad you all got my email."

A ripple of laughter passed through the gathered students.

"Seriously, though," Laurent continued, "I'm really happy you're all here. I know what it's like to have things happen that you can't explain, or that you *could*, but people would think you were crazy. I know how that can be—exciting and isolating all at once. And I definitely know what it's like to learn to actually use that power that you can't fully admit is real."

Mia glanced around the room, saw the nodding, the recognition on other faces, knew it was on hers, too.

"We'll have time to go into all of that, but for now, I know why you're here. So let's do some magic." He opened a box of pencils, then, with a sharp wave of his hand, caused seven of them to fly out and land on the occupied desks.

From the back of the room: "Oh, fuck yes."

Laurent laughed. "Something like that."

He shifted into teacher mode then and explained that all spells had some component that would help the magician focus their energy and intent. Levitation was a spell that relied on gesture, rather than words, for its focus, for example. Mia shaped her fingers into the same sharp-angled bends as Mr. Beauchamps'. A thrill ran beneath her skin, nervous, electric. She focused on the pencil in front of her.

It leapt into the air.

A half laugh bubbled up, and the pencil bobbed along with it. Mia made herself breathe in slowly, calmly, and as she settled, so did the magic.

The pencil hovering in the air. A lightness just beneath her skin. A sense of potential, waiting.

It felt amazing.

"Congratulations," Laurent said. "Welcome to the Unseen World."

The Unseen World. It had a name. And she belonged in it. Mia lowered the pencil back to the desk. "Cool. What's next?"

A pencil flew past him, close enough that Laurent could smell that it had been freshly sharpened, fast enough that it buried itself an inch deep in the corkboard he'd been standing in front of. A petite girl with burnt-umber skin and flashes of lime green woven into her hair looked at him with a mix of glee and horror on her face. "Sorry, Mr. B. Forgot to focus."

He laughed. "At least you missed."

Laurent couldn't remember the last time he felt so happy about the existence of magic. Not glad he had it, or aware of its usefulness, but just happy. Maybe when he was a kid, when it was still uncomplicated—just something cool and special. Before it had become duels to the death and struggles for power and secrets he wished he could unknow. Back when it had only been possibility. The faces around him reflected that utter joy and delight in discovery that he remembered.

A cackle of laughter from the back of the room and Laurent looked over to see a Latino boy holding up hands that were a vividly iridescent blue. "I think I need magic remover. Or gloves."

"Let's see what we can do."

CHAPTER FIVE

After weeks of effort, House Merlin was—as much as she could make it in mundane fashion—fully Lara's now. There was new furniture, new paint on the walls, even new carpet in two of the rooms. She had removed all the technology her father had put in place to maintain the illusion that he still had magic. Everything that had been specifically his was gone.

It had felt like trying to unhaunt a house. She had cleaned out and changed everything that had been connected to him, making it a place where no trace of his could linger.

That had been a good, necessary first step, but it was only a first step. Now she would see if she could make House Merlin hers magically as well.

She wanted the connection, the magical link that was possible between the Head of House and the physical building. Not so much because it would be an extension of her own power—though it would be nice to have the House be able to perform basic tasks on its own—but as an acknowledgment of responsibility. It would be a sign that the House was fully bound to her, and she to it. She needed that binding in order to truly feel like she held the House, with all that entailed.

Under normal circumstances, she would have had a starting point to establish that link. There would have also been records kept by the House itself, records of residents, of spells done that had drawn on the House's magic, of the pieces of life that the House had been part of. Lara would have been able to speak to the House directly, ask questions about what she needed to know. But Miles hadn't had enough magic to maintain that connection for years, and everything that might have once been part of it was lost. She would need to build it again.

"Here goes nothing," she murmured.

Lara stood just inside the front door, facing the House as if she had just entered it. She took a deep breath to steady herself and then opened her hands, palms out and fingers extended, and *reached*.

The spell was a cool breeze. Curtains waved as it passed, and the sharp, clear scent of lemon and rosemary lingered in its wake.

Her magic searched through all of House Merlin—through floors and hallways, through walls and wiring. Through every board and nail, every fleck of paint. Looking for some sort of connection, some spark of awareness for her magic to mesh with.

And there was nothing.

No magic.

Not anywhere.

It was as if the House was a mundane building, had always

been a mundane building, and nothing more. There was not even enough residual magic for her to sense where it had been.

Lara shook her hands to loosen them, then tried again, reaching through the House. After a few minutes, she broke off the spell, swore.

Nothing.

She'd known Miles had been a poor steward of the House, but she hadn't expected this complete absence of magic. The totality of it. She had expected a remnant, a memory, that something left in the House would recognize what it had once been, what she was trying to bring it back to.

Lara slumped in the doorway.

She could still do this. She knew there were procedures in place for when a new House was established. Ian's friend Laurent was dealing with those, and she knew he'd talk to her about it, tell her what needed doing or who to ask for help. But it was so embarrassing—a magicless founding House. One more way in which Miles hadn't been what he'd pretended to be, what he should have been. She'd thought she'd cleared everything of his from the House, but his failure remained, a smear over everything else.

Less disconcerting than her constant physical awareness of the Houses, but far more annoying, was the paperwork that came with being the Head of the Unseen World. In fact, if she had to pick, Grace would have chosen the latter as being her least favorite part. The map of the Houses over her body stayed the same. The paperwork kept getting worse.

Miles Merlin had been in charge her entire life. He'd been the one to shut her away in Shadows as part of a cover-up. So Grace hadn't spent a lot of time considering what the actual job of being the Head of the Unseen World was. At first she hadn't really cared, and then her only example was corrupt.

Miles hadn't left any helpful notes for his successor. She suspected that he hadn't planned to have one. Either that, or the paperwork and administrivia had been a curse he'd been happy to pass on.

Maybe that.

Seemingly everyone in the Unseen World had something they wanted to complain about, and all of them directed their complaints to her.

The complaints had begun almost as soon as the Turning had ended. Issues of precedence and ranking among the newly ordered Houses, what the establishment of House Beauchamps meant, what would happen to the magic from the House of Shadows. What had happened to the House of Shadows. What was the Unseen World supposed to do now, without it.

Most were petty grievances, things she could and did ignore. The complaints around Shadows were different. Those, she paid attention to. It was clear from the beginning that what Sydney had done wasn't going to be seen as a needed break from a horrific past but rather as an interregnum. It would only be a matter of time before one of the people who was sure that Shadows should be brought back would attempt to actually do that. Once people realized that the House itself was still connected to magic, was restructuring itself, that attempt would come even sooner.

Espresso in hand, Grace sat at her desk. "What do I have today?" she asked House Prospero.

Her computer monitor woke up, revealing a number of emails that would have appalled her previously but now only made her wince a little. The drawer where she kept her physical correspondence remained thankfully closed. She had set up the spells early on, after the House had asked what it could do to help her. The investment of magic had paid itself back in the fact that she hadn't torn out her hair while trying to stay organized.

The tight scrawl of her handwriting appeared on the surface of her desk mirror: *Do you want to see the House of Shadows?*

She didn't, not really, but if the House was asking, it was best that she check in. "Yes, thank you."

The globe next to her desk began to spin, becoming increasingly transparent as it did. Once it was clear as glass, it paused its movement. A flash of dark smoke filled the sphere, then cleared to reveal an aerial view of the island where the House of Shadows waited.

There was more of it now. Still unorganized, still misshapen heaps and clumps, but more. More where there should have been none. It seemed, too, as she watched, that it had become faster in the way it moved and connected itself together, as if the spell that was animating it was growing stronger.

She couldn't feel it directly, not yet. The number of Houses that had mapped themselves over her body hadn't changed. She worried it was only a matter of time before it would.

"Thank you," she told the House, and the globe unspun until it was itself again.

The one good thing about beginning her day with a self-regenerating horror was that it made confronting her inbox feel a little less dire.

She hadn't even opened the first message before a gentle chime from the House interrupted her.

Catriona Don would like to see you.

Grace sat back, considering. Catriona didn't have an appointment, but from what she remembered of her at school, she wasn't the kind of person who would consider appointments necessary. For that alone, she almost refused. But she suspected she knew why Catriona was there.

"I'll see her, thank you."

The House showed the other woman in, its magic opening doors and offering a gentle sense of which way to turn in halls.

Catriona fixed her gaze firmly on Grace as she seated herself in one of the guest chairs on the opposite side of the desk. "Look, this bullshit has gone on long enough."

"And good morning to you, too."

"Oh, come off it. You know why I'm here. Just because your House seems to be holding together doesn't mean you don't know what's going on with the others."

"I do, yes." She offered no more than the minimum, curious to see how Catriona would fill in the gap.

"The Houses are falling apart, literally. As of this morning, one of the chimneys in House Don is an empty column with a pile of dust at the bottom, and that's only the second-most annoying thing that's happened this week. When are you going to do something about it?"

"I'm very sorry to hear that, but the Houses and their maintenance are the responsibilities of the individual magicians. There isn't anything that I can do."

"You are the Head of the Unseen World." Catriona spoke slowly, in a manner that suggested she thought Grace needed reminding.

"I'm afraid that doesn't change anything."

"It means that you're the one who could make sure we all get the magic that's rightfully ours," Catriona said.

Grace didn't like seeing the scars that the House of Shadows had left on her. They were a too-direct reminder of something she would never forget. But she let the illusion she usually wore fall away so that they showed against her skin. "Rightfully?" she repeated.

Catriona sighed. "Obviously, you were never meant to be in there. I'm not suggesting that. But look. We all know things were better before."

"We do?"

"Houses weren't falling apart, and people didn't have to bleed for their magic, so yes, we do."

"I had to bleed for your magic, Catriona. So did Sydney, and Verenice. Countless people died for it. So no, I don't think things were better before. I do, however, think we're done here.

"The House will show you out."

Every day began and ended with the candles. Lighting them, then trying to extinguish the flames. She was stuck, stalled. Sydney wouldn't allow herself anything other than certainty, and she was only certain that she could extinguish a candle three times out of ten.

It wasn't enough. Shadows was growing. Becoming more coherent, rising in power. Becoming itself once more.

She was not.

She might have almost been able to bear her own lack of power if she hadn't also been aware that Shadows continued to grow stronger. It felt like magic had chosen between them, and she had lost. That she had failed.

She couldn't allow that failure. Not when she knew what Shadows was.

She sat at her kitchen table, guttered votive tins scattered around her, the air still thick with the scents of cheap burnt wax and smoke, and stared at her hands. Magician's hands. Nails kept short, fingers wiry with muscle from a lifetime of spells, skin crosshatched by scars.

Scars that meant magic. Scars where magic had been cut from her bones. Bones that still held magic. Magic that someone else could use, if her bones were no longer inside her.

Sydney walked over to her counter and picked up a knife.

A paring knife. Small, easy to handle. Barely a weight at all in her hand. The scrape of the blade against the sharpener smooth, almost meditative. It would be better if it were sharp.

She struck. Fast. Unflinching. All the way to bone.

The scars from Shadows were patterns already written on her skin. All she had to do was follow them.

She traced the knife through skin, flesh, bone. Blood welled in the wake of the blade. She cut harder, deeper, waited for the spark, the flare of magic to pass from her bone through the knife.

Waited and waited and waited.

Nothing.

She slid the knife from her arm and dropped it, clattering, in the sink. A towel, wrapped tight to stop the bleeding. Disinfectant and gauze and tape and a clumsy mess of bandaging, rather than the swift ease of a healing spell.

Sydney washed her blood from her counters, her floor, from her own hands.

From the knife, which she then dried and replaced in the block.

She gathered the empty candle tins and threw them away. Straightened a chair that had been knocked askew. Then she sank, slowly, to the floor, curled her arms around herself, and wept.

CHAPTER SIX

It was barely morning. Mist hung in the air, dampening her skin as Dahlia walked through Central Park. Dew, heavy on the grass, soaked through the edges of her shoes. Chill sank in with it, a cold that settled in her bones.

She was here to learn what—if anything—was left of the House of Shadows. To see what would be needed to rebuild, to return magic to it. To make it as it should have been, had it been free from Miles Merlin's theft and treachery.

As she walked, she passed through the new, strangely grown trees. The bone trees bloomed with voices. Each different from the previous, the stories reaching out as Dahlia walked past. Tales of loss, tales of longing, tales of loneliness. The dawning breeze rustled the leaves, set the petals of the bone flowers chiming against themselves like glass shattering. She'd been told they were the dead. These trees and their hearts of bone and their speaking sorrows. The dead of the Unseen World, rising up in new shapes as a reminder.

A reminder of what? she wondered. Those who opposed Shadows would hear these voices as lines in a tragedy, or as a warning against letting the House return.

But she heard them as a warning as well—a warning about what happened when power was wasted, when sacrifices were taken for granted.

Even though everyone in the Unseen World had known about the House of Shadows, had participated in it, it had been treated like some sort of dirty secret. The House itself, hidden away here, rather than someplace where it would be seen and known. That hiddenness had been part of what made it so easy for Miles to corrupt its purpose and steal its power for his own.

If the proper amount of magic had been available, could Rose have fought back against Grey? Dahlia stopped to consider, the voices in the background of her thoughts.

". . . no one to remember . . ."

". . . she never even said my name . . ."

"But it's not a House, it's a prison."

No. Even then, impossible. The purpose of Shadows had only been to take away consequences, not to increase magic for those who were weaker magicians. She loved Rose, but her sister's magic had not been strong.

". . . no family but there . . ."

". . . taken and then forgotten . . ."

". . . my magic bleeding out of me."

The trees smelled like mourning. The salt and heat of tears, the cold staleness of bone, the dust of a room empty for too long. The back of Dahlia's throat ached as she walked.

What wouldn't she give to hear Rose one more time, even like this, just a voice among the trees? She had kept Rose's room as it had been for three months after her death. Then, one morning, Dahlia had walked in, and even though everything was still exactly as it had been, even though nothing visible had changed, that day it had only been an empty room, no trace left of Rose.

That was the day that Dahlia had asked the House to close the room away, seal it off. There was no doorway on that side of the hall now, but she still knew exactly where to knock.

". . . alone . . . alone . . . alone."

"In Shadows. As if that helps."

". . . don't want to be forgotten."

Dahlia agreed that those who had gone as sacrifices deserved to be remembered and more directly than they were. It was clear that the Unseen World didn't function without Shadows. It needed to be returned to power. Not just returned, but made more. The spell modified, so that those who needed it could use the magic generated. That should be possible. She would make it so it was.

The reservoir came into view, and Dahlia froze. Then laughed, bright and triumphant.

There was no need to go to the island to determine if magic remained. She could see that it did from here, as stone moved toward stone, as pieces of a wall came together before her eyes. Magic itself knew that the House of Shadows was necessary to the Unseen World: Here it was, remaking it.

It was slow, uneven. Things moved at random, did not always match up with what they found or ran into. But they *moved.*

Dahlia barely heard the trees as she left the park.

"So," Sydney said, "tell me about these kids you've been working with." The bright morning air in Laurent's apartment smelled of cinnamon and coffee. Mimosas sparkled on the table next to bowls of tiny strawberries. She watched the city through his windows, sun-streaked and shining at this height. "Breakfast is as amazing as usual, by the way."

"Thanks," Laurent said. "There's nine of them now that show up regularly and about five more that pop in and out. Junior high, high school. From all over the city. It's exactly what I hoped for."

"And it makes you really happy." It was easy to see in the broadness of his smile, the expansiveness of his gestures as he spoke.

"It does. Like, this feels like a thing I *should* be doing with all this power and status, not just looking to build a new, expensive house. Or House, I should say." He rolled his eyes at the proper noun.

"Still haven't picked a place?"

Laurent tried on an expression of exaggerated innocence. "Sydney, I don't even know when I'll find the time. I've just been so busy with all these new obligations that are part of the Unseen World."

She laughed. "Doing actual important work, you mean?"

"I know it sounds silly, but these kids, bringing them in and making a place for them—this is how we change things. They're how we make the Unseen World into what it should be. This is how we make sure that things like the House of Shadows never happen again."

"It doesn't sound silly, not at all. It sounds necessary," Sydney said. The lines of her face sharpened, drew in. "Unfortunately, particularly so right now."

"What?" Laurent asked.

"Shadows." An entire world in that word. "I don't think there are magicians involved, not yet, and I don't know if that makes this better or worse, but the House of Shadows—the literal, physical place—is trying to come back," she explained.

Laurent leaned back in his chair. "On its own seems less bad than under someone's direction? None of it sounds great, but at least it's not someone trying to go back to how things were."

"I think it's less organized, not less bad. And I think that someone directing it is a when, not an if," Sydney said. "People will find out, if they haven't already, and there are enough people in the Unseen World who thought Shadows was a good idea that someone will decide to help what's going on out there along."

Laurent considered for a moment, then shook his head. "I wish I disagreed with you. People are really fucked up.

"So what's being done to stop it? There's a plan, right?"

"Well, I am going to the archives to do research, as that's all I'm good for, but if you have any other ideas as to what I can do without any magic, I'd love to hear them." Sydney spat the words like acid.

"Syd, I didn't mean you should go out there by yourself."

"I'm sorry. That wasn't fair. I just feel useless right now, like all I can do is stand back and watch the disaster unfold." She pressed her hand over her eyes, and her sleeve fell back to reveal her arm covered in bandages.

"Are you okay right now?" His eyes on the splotches of red that showed through the gauze.

"I don't even know what okay is right now, Laurent. You said you had a question, something you wanted to talk to me about. Ask it. Please. Give me something to do. It's easier when I'm doing something." She got up and walked to the window, stared out over the city.

"If I can do anything . . ." He let the words trail off, leaving a space for her fill if she wanted.

"I'll tell you," she lied.

He waited one more beat, then: "All right. It goes back to this House I'm supposed to be building. I've been getting these emails and stuff, and, well, they're—actually, it will be easier if I show you." He pulled up a folder from his inbox and handed her his tablet.

Sydney sat next to him as she scrolled scrolled through the messages. "Did you run a keyword search on these?"

"Yes. There are twenty-three mentions of bones or skeletons in eleven emails. I couldn't tell if it was just me, or if—"

"Or if it seems like the Unseen World wants you to immure someone in your new House."

"Yeah. And quite frankly, Syd, I was planning on going in a different direction with my interior decorating."

A smile flickered over her face. "I'll bet."

"But seriously, why is this so important? I know these people are into all sorts of sketchy and weird shit, but there's usually something that at least pretends to be a reason for it. I cannot figure out what possible reason there is for sticking Great-Uncle Wallace in the foundations."

She cocked her head. "Do you have a Great-Uncle Wallace?"

"No. But even if I did, I would not be about to dig the poor man up and stick him in a wall in my House."

"No. Obviously not." Sydney leaned back, lost in thought. Then: "Bones."

"Right, skeletons in the foundations."

"No, I mean that's the why. The bones. Magic lingers in bones—the bones of the fingers and hands most of all, because that's where the way we cast spells makes it concentrate."

"Which is why Grey took them from the women he murdered."

Sydney nodded. "But any magician's skeleton—the entirety of it—would be full of residual magic. It's why the House of Shadows was built on bones. All of the remains of the sacrifices who died there were kept on the island—it's part of how the House powered itself and probably where it's drawing the energy from to rebuild. I'm guessing having relics in the foundations of the Houses of the Unseen World is based on the same principles of magic."

She paused. "No, not based on. The original. Bones in the foundations of the Houses is where they got the idea to build Shadows like they did."

"Okay—and gross—but I still don't get why I need a skeleton for my House." Laurent shuddered.

"Because the House is connected to the magician that holds it. It's that link that gives the House power to act on its own. But that's a really big spell, and one that's meant to be continuous. To last through the life of the House. So it needs some sort of anchor. If you're anchoring it in a source of magic, that adds strength to the connection and to the spell. It becomes more stable. I bet the older Houses all used the bones of family members, too, just to maximize the magical potential."

"Like I said before, gross."

"There'd be records," Sydney said. "I can check the archives for them when I'm there."

"I'll see if I can get any of these helpful people to be a bit more specific as to who exactly it is I'm supposed to immure in my House," Laurent said. "You know, I really had hoped we were done with the horrifically weird."

"Welcome to the Unseen World," Sydney said. "There's no place like home."

Instead of going back to her apartment after breakfast with Laurent, Sydney went to House Prospero. The conversation had raised questions she wanted to see if the House had answers to.

After she'd said hello to Grace and the House, and reassured them both that she was well, she asked, "Do you remember being built?"

The answer scrawled across the surface of the mirror.

I was built before I was myself.

So the structure predated the spell. That made sense, especially with the spell needing a physical anchor. "Do you remember becoming yourself?"

Which time?

That was unexpected. She turned to Grace. "Has Prospero ever moved physical Houses?"

"It hasn't. But I'm not sure what else that could mean. Do you want me to check the House records?"

"If you don't mind."

Sydney addressed the House again. "The first time, I think."

I became all at once.

"At the completion of the spell, then." It made sense. A spell that large would have been built in pieces, the magic layered together, and only kindled once everything was in place.

"Was there, at that time, a place in your structure where you felt specifically connected? To your magician, or to yourself?"

I was everywhere.

"I understand." She'd try a little less metaphorical query. "There may be someone inside of your structure. Placed in your walls or under your floors, perhaps. They'd be only bones now. Can you sense if there is?"

"There is what?" Grace hissed.

The surface of the mirror remained blank as the House thought. Then: *If there is, I cannot sense them as anything other than myself.*

"All right. Thank you for answering my questions."

"Sydney?" Grace asked, a hint of impatience coloring her voice.

"I was talking with Laurent about his House, and it made me think of anchors for spells. Bones in the foundations, that sort of thing. Which, yes, you probably have here somewhere. But I was thinking in terms of Shadows, and what that meant. If we could find the anchor out there on the island, maybe we can break the spell, and stop it from coming back."

A chime from the mirror: *When you gave me your magic, Sydney, when I became your House. That was the second time I became myself.*

"You gave House Prospero your magic?"

"Some. Not a lot. It had magic from Shadows in its animating spell. I replaced it. I didn't want it here, not if the House was mine. I didn't know that mattered to the House."

It did.

CHAPTER SEVEN

Sydney sat in her kitchen and wiped blood from beneath her nose. She swallowed hard against the rise of nausea in her throat. Four out of ten. That was how many candles she was sure she had put out with magic. Four. More than a week ago. It was progress.

It wasn't nearly enough.

She'd had bones broken, when she had been in Shadows. Knew the deep, sticky-sweet ache of shattered bone knitting back together. There were times she thought she felt the same bone-deep stirring when she put out the candles, like something emergent, waiting. She didn't have time to wait.

It was an added layer of spite that even without magic of her own, she could feel the House of Shadows like a tumor at the base of her skull, growing, and growing stronger. The clinging, lurking feeling haunted her, there when she got out of bed in the morning, and there at night when she tried to sleep. Always, always, a veil tangled over her thoughts.

She wanted it gone. Gone for good this time. The limb amputated, the rot cut out. She had to make herself strong enough to do that.

She took out another candle.

"Sydney! What are you doing?" Ian pushed a handful of tissues at her, mopped at the blood spattered on the table.

She hadn't heard him come in, didn't know how long he had been watching. "What does it look like I'm doing?" She set the tissues to the side, clearing the space for her work.

"Besides bleeding?" His eyes went to the tracery of healing scabs on her left arm. "And making yourself bleed on purpose, apparently. What the fuck, Syd?"

Sydney cut her eyes sideways at him. "Better to bleed than to do nothing."

"Is it really?" Ian cleaned guttered votive tins from the table, sweeping them into the trash. "I know you're worried about Shadows, but there are other magicians. Even assuming it rebuilds successfully, and then assuming that something were to happen beyond that to cause its magic to come back in some kind of meaningful way, and then something else were to happen to put people under its power again—which, by the way, is a lot to assume—you don't need to be the one to save everyone."

"I had to before." Before. A world of time encompassed in that word.

"You had magic then." He turned away from her and began making coffee, as if her loss was an end to the conversation. For him, it was. Things were neat for him. A before and after, not an ongoing ache. Not something to be fought against.

"So did you, when you learned what Shadows was." She watched him continue to not understand.

"Right. And after I learned that, I made certain the magic that I used was my own. I stopped using the magic that came from Shadows once I knew its origin. I went to Verenice to relearn how to be a magician without it. You know that."

"What else did you do?" Quiet.

He closed a cupboard and turned to look at her, confusion in every line of his face. "What?"

"When you found out about the source of the magic that came from Shadows," Sydney said slowly, taking care to be precise with her words, "what else did you do? Because it was your family that built that place and created that magic that bound the Unseen World to it. Your family who came up with the idea to put people like me there to be used up so that they could cast a spell without paying the consequences for it. It was your aunt who left these scars on my arms as she carved magic out of me. Your father who corrupted the spell so much that the only way to end it cost me my magic.

"And even if none of those things had been true, it was still a horror that you discovered. That you knew about. That you watched your family and friends participate in every time they used magic. So I am asking you, what else did you do? You know, to end it."

Ian stood, silent.

"Exactly," Sydney said. "People built that place and its magic on purpose. They let it run for generations. Even the people who admitted that it was wrong did nothing besides quietly accept that this was just the way things were, and that was really sad, but nothing that could be changed.

"So what makes you think that someone else will step up this time if it needs to be stopped? No one did before. Not one. Not ever. Not even you.

"I could ask you what you're doing now, too, Ian. Now that you know it's trying to come back, but you've already told me. You're assuming it won't happen, and you're going about your life.

"I can't do that.

"That's why I'm bleeding. That's why I tried to cut magic out of myself like your aunt cut it out of me in the House of Shadows. Because I will do anything, *anything* I can to make sure Shadows doesn't actually rebuild itself and recast the spells it was made of. Even if the only magic I can do is lighting candles so that I have something to see by as I take apart every stone on that island by hand."

He stepped forward as if he might reach for her, then froze as she grabbed tissues, pressed them to her nose. The white bloomed red. Ian shook his head. "I can't do this. I can't just sit here and watch you bleed, Syd."

"Then don't." She threw the stained tissue away, then took out another candle. She spoke the word that lit it.

After a moment, Sydney heard her door open and then close.

"I thought you were going to install some sort of doorbell spell."

Lara startled at her brother's unexpected appearance in her kitchen. "Ian! Fuck! I didn't even hear you come in."

"I texted to let you know I was on my way."

"'On my way' is not in the kitchen, Ian!"

"Like I said, I thought you were putting in a doorbell spell. What happened with that?"

"What happened is there's no magic left in this House to anchor it. Zip. Zero. Nothing." She could cast something basic, like a ward, that didn't require the House to be able to communicate with her, but nothing more than that.

"Oh."

She rolled her eyes. "That's one way of putting it."

"None? No magic at all?"

"None, Ian. I checked. More than once. The House has no more magic than Miles did." She heaved a sigh. "Let's start again. Hello, brother dear. So nice to see you. What brings you to my unspelled door this evening?"

He didn't even crack a smile at the attempted levity, but looked tired, preoccupied. "I need to pick up some of the things I left in the room here. I'm going away for a bit. It won't take me long to grab them."

She blinked, perplexed. "But you just brought that stuff over. Like, literally two days ago. What's up?"

"I had a fight with Sydney. A big one. She's hurting herself, pushing too hard to get her magic back, and I can't stay here and watch."

"So you're leaving. Of course."

"What does that mean?"

"Well, it's what you do, isn't it? You leave. Every time something gets hard, you go. That's what you did all the time growing up. I was actually shocked you came back for the Turning. I guess what I should have been was surprised that you stayed this long."

"What am I supposed to do? Stand around doing nothing? Just watch while someone I care about hurts herself?"

Lara stared at her brother. "You get that there are options that land in between doing nothing and running away, right? You could actually stay here and try."

"Try what?"

"I don't know, Ian. I'm not the one who needs to figure that out. But if you can't, or won't, then fine. Go get your stuff. The room will still be here for you when things are easy again."

Do something. Ian strode through the darkening light of Central Park. *Do something. All you do is leave.* Sydney's and Lara's voices alternated in his head.

He wasn't even sure there was something to be done at this point, but he would go to the island and see what was there.

It wasn't as if he had never done anything. He had cut himself off from the magic of Shadows; he had rebuilt his own without it. Maybe that wasn't enough for some people, but it wasn't nothing.

He had left to show he wouldn't be part of a world that relied on Shadows, had come back to stand against it in the Turning—that had been a condition of his contract with Miranda Prospero. There was a purpose in what he had done. It hadn't been just running away.

He came to the shore of the reservoir. A small wooden boat waited. It looked ancient, as if an overly large ripple would send it to pieces, and there was standing water in the bow. He stepped in and urged it in the direction of the island with a whispered phrase and an abbreviated wave of his left hand.

Night had fallen by the time he stepped onto the island. He opened the flashlight app on his phone and, for a moment, thought he smelled the plastic vanilla scent of Sydney's candles.

A scrape like a horror movie sound effect to his left, and part of a wall dragged itself toward him. He watched it stutter and shake as it made its way over the earth. He hadn't fully realized what it had meant for Sydney to have fought the House of Shadows, to have cast the kind of magic that turned this building into a ruin, while the building—the House itself and all the magic at its disposal—had fought back.

During the Turning, if their challenge hadn't been interrupted, she would have killed him.

The ground shifted beneath him, some sort of lump rising under his feet, and Ian stumbled, falling to his knees. He hissed at his abraded palms as he stood back up, wiping blood and dirt on his jeans.

More movement around him, then, the groans and stretches of stone seeking stone.

He wondered if he could stop them. The House was broken already. Even though there was movement, magic, present, everything here was disorganized and half-done.

A stasis spell, maybe. An extended one, large enough to hold whatever magic was here, to keep it from coming back. But before that, some way of making sure there were no pieces of the original House for the magic to come back to.

Ian considered for a moment, then bent his hands into claws, right above left. He pulled, slowly, moving his hands in opposing directions. As he did, he spoke words of separation in slow syllables, their pieces falling from his lips like grit.

Matching claw marks appeared on the stone closest to him. He watched as the marks sank deeper and deeper, the stone crumbling into pieces. Into dust that mingled with the earth as if it had never been anything else.

A smile spread across his face as the stone disintegrated. Good. He could do this. He just needed to expand the scope of the spell.

He sank his hands into the ground, reaching through the pile of dust that had once been part of the House of Shadows. Shifted his hands into the clawed shapes. Focused his magic.

A grasping, tugging tear from the earth beneath him.

Before anything registered, even the pain, that same strange tearing once more.

Pain then. Huge and impossible, turning the world red.

His hands.

Gone.

The House of Shadows, the magic on this cursed island, had taken his hands. Reeling wildly, Ian stumbled back toward the water. To the boat. His vision tunneled.

Barely conscious, he tripped over the side of the boat and fell into it. His last thought before darkness swallowed him was that he could cast no magic to bring himself home.

CHAPTER EIGHT

This time, there was a funeral. A sun-shot grey sky over an open wound in the ground. Rows of black-clad mourners and spills of white flowers.

Sydney watched as Lara's handful of dirt spattered across the shining surface of the coffin. Verenice, standing next to Sydney, gulped back a sob. Laurent, on her other side, quietly wept. Tears had streamed down Lara's face as she eulogized her brother, telling stories of their childhood, of his kindness to her, of how his presence had made her feel less alone. Sydney hadn't cried yet. She wasn't sure if she could.

Ian had still been alive when she had found him.

Just before dawn, she'd felt the clawed presence of Shadows that lurked at the back of her neck clench in glee. She'd known that something had happened, and so she had gone there in the morning's breaking light, drawn as if Shadows still had the power to summon her.

She had broken into a run when she saw the boat, only partially on the shore. Had fallen to her knees beside it when she saw what it contained. "Ian."

He was so still, so wounded, she thought he was dead.

Hand trembling, she'd brushed the hair out of his eyes, then gasped as they'd fluttered open.

"Syd." His voice ragged, quiet. "So sorry. Tried."

"I know, Ian. I know."

It had been the last thing he said. She felt the House of Shadows laughing.

"Sydney." Laurent's voice recalled her to herself. It was her turn to step forward, to throw her handful of dirt onto the coffin.

It seemed so strange that the Unseen World buried their dead. Buried them in coffins that locked away the magic that remained in a magician's bones. It was so unlike Shadows.

Shadows had kept a part of Ian, though. Stolen his hands and all their magic and kept them.

Sydney's skin felt too hot, too tight.

"Sydney, Miranda is here. I'm going to say hello, if you want to join me." Verenice had, Sydney knew, spoken with her mother after the other woman had been stripped of her magic. Sydney looked over, met Miranda's eyes, then turned away. "No, I don't have anything to say to her."

She wanted, desperately, to be anywhere else.

Her heels sank into the grass as she walked over to Lara, everything askew, off-kilter. "I am so sorry," she said, knowing the words were inadequate, not knowing any others.

"He was going to leave." Lara was almost transparently pale against the black of her suit, the fuchsia shock of her hair.

Smudges like bruises beneath her eyes the only color in her skin. "He was going to leave, and I told him to stay and do something."

"I'm sorry." The words even more useless on a second utterance.

Sydney stepped out of the line of condolences, walked as fast as she could away from Lara and the crowd and the scar of the grave. From Verenice and Laurent and well-meaning words. Walked, wishing she could keep walking until it didn't hurt anymore.

Miles Merlin did not attend.

CHAPTER NINE

Madison had asked Sydney if she wanted to reschedule her visit to the archives. "No. If Shadows could do that, could fight Ian, it's more connected to magic than I thought. And his death"—she paused, swallowed hard—"the circumstances of his death will mean that people know that Shadows is functioning on its own. It's going to be harder to stop them from helping it."

So she was there, the day after the funeral, in the offices of Wellington & Ketchum.

"Thanks for coming with me." Sydney nodded in the direction of the elevator as she and Harper waited for its doors to open. "Madison says this will go more smoothly if you're there."

What they were looking for was an origin story. All of the law firms with Unseen World clients kept records that dated back to the founding, and that included the original plans for the Houses. In those would be what was necessary for the creation of a House—the mundane things, like bills of sale and blueprints, and the more magical, the required set of spells necessary to make them part of the Unseen World, the reasons for the bones in the walls, and the thing that connected the Houses magically. But the archives were their own highly idiosyncratic and mutable filing system, one that was perfectly capable of hiding material that they didn't want found.

"I hope so. The archives have their moods," Harper said. "Are you sure you don't want to do the access spells? You do have a lot more experience."

Wellington & Ketchum's archives were on the thirty-ninth floor of a building that usually only had thirty-eight. They contained the files that were too important to entrust to the law firm's computer system—judgments that had been magically rendered, or spelled files, or simply secrets that the firm's more mundane lawyers didn't need access to. Getting onto that floor involved successfully performing a series of spells. These spells were stored in objects that required only specific knowledge, rather than independent magical ability to activate, and the rules of the archives meant that every magician who entered was required to use the stored spells, rather than their own magic.

"You're more used to going into the archives. And since, from what I understand, messing up the spells means that the place self-destructs, I'm just as happy to let you handle things."

Harper nodded. "That's valid."

The elevator doors slid open, and the two women stepped in. Harper used a plastic access card that had been cut into the shape of a physical key to override the system and trigger the path to the thirty-ninth floor. The elevator paused for a second, dropped half a foot, then flung itself upward.

"Is it always that dramatic?" Sydney asked.

"Sometimes," Harper said. "Even when things work, the archives sort of decide how well."

The elevator slammed to a halt, and the doors opened on what seemed to be an empty concrete warehouse. Sydney raised a brow but didn't otherwise move.

Harper took a small clear box from her pocket and tapped the lid three times. Pink, cotton-candy-scented smoke curled out, canceling the magical self-destruct sequence, and undoing the wards that hid the room's true nature. When the smoke cleared, the archives looked like the large, elegant room that they were. Rows and rows of files in various kinds of storage, partially illuminated by floor-to-ceiling windows, interspersed with a riot of green plants.

"This next bit is my least favorite part." Harper walked to a table at the center of the room. On it was a small white candle. She picked it up and whispered the words of the spell, the one piece of all of this that required newly cast magic. The candle lit and with it so did the sconces on the walls and a large, ornate chandelier that hung from the ceiling. Harper set the candle down and pinched the bridge of her nose. "Headache. Every time."

Sydney nodded. "I know how that goes. So, what's the filing system here?"

"System?"

"Where do I start looking?" The walls were lined with possibilities, cabinets and flat storage, open shelving and locked cases. More storage arranged itself in the open part of the room, a forest of history awaiting a bread-crumb trail.

"Remember how I said the archives have a mind of their own? That mind has a very . . . unique organizational system. The candle spell helps sometimes. It might turn on a particular set of lights near where a file is, but 'might' is the key word there."

"Ah. When Madison asked me to make those stored locator spells, I didn't quite realize how much location was needed. Are there any left?"

"There might be," Harper said. "I wasn't sure how you'd feel about using them, since they were your magic."

One more thing she would have to get over. "Let's use them next time. Anything to make this easier. For now, I suppose, just start looking and hope the archives like me?"

"Pretty much."

Before either of them moved, a wind, strong enough to rattle drawers and light fixtures, blew through the room, extinguishing the candle Harper had lit.

"Harper?"

"No, that doesn't usually happen."

"So is now when we worry?" Sydney's voice polite, conversational.

A pop as the chandelier above her went out. Darkness fell

to cover Sydney like a cloak. She could feel it, a heavy velvet plush that clung to her skin, almost like a shadow. A memory of magic deep in her bones. Flashes, firefly green, at the edge of her vision.

"Not quite yet. Let's just both head back to the elevator." Harper, voice deliberately calm, but Sydney could feel tension radiating from her.

With a bang, file drawers shot open, their contents spraying across the room as if an errant poltergeist had passed through. The wind picked up loose papers, spun them tighter and tighter in circles.

Harper pressed the button for the elevator. Nothing happened. She pressed it again, with the same lack of response. "Okay, now. Now is when we worry."

"The candle." Sydney ran to the table, picked it up. It was just possible that restarting that piece of the spell, offering her own magic, might act as a check on the chaos.

White flame shot from the candle, which melted into nothingness. The wind moaned, and the room grew darker still.

"Sydney, we need to go." Harper had jammed her fingers into the seam of the elevator doors and was straining to pull them open.

Sydney stepped toward Harper, toward the elevator, then stopped. "A mind of their own?"

The wind howled loud enough that Harper had to yell to be heard over it. "What?"

"The archives. You said they had a mind of their own."

"Yes, and, Sydney, right now that mind *hates* us. We need to go!"

"No, it's just a child, throwing a tantrum, and it needs to stop it." Sydney turned toward the chaos that was the flat files, papers worn with age scattered in heaps and tumbling across the floor, and shouted, "Enough!"

The air crackled around her, acid-green flashes of heat lightning. "Enough," she said again. "You're right. Something has gone wrong with magic. I can feel it, too, the rot in it, the missing pieces and imbalance. I don't like it any more than you do. But we are trying to fix whatever it is that's wrong—to set things right. I think you have the answers here, or at least the means of discovering them. So you can either keep your files tucked away, and throw them around in such a mess that even you don't know where they are anymore, or you can behave, and let us work, and maybe we can put this right."

Harper could feel the room itself pause and consider—the sensation of a match caught between the strike and the flame.

The lights rose. Drawers and doors that had been flung open shut themselves. The contents of shelves moved back into semiorganized lines.

"All right, then," Sydney said. "That's better. Thank you."

On knees that felt like water, Harper walked over to the nearest set of files and began putting things back together.

In the aftermath, the archives smelled of stone and beeswax and smoke, as if a great breath had simultaneously extinguished all the candles of a cathedral. It was not, Harper thought, a particularly comforting scent, in a place this full of paper, paper currently scattered and tossed about by the archives itself.

Nothing about what had just happened was particularly comforting, though. She could still taste the burnt ozone of strong magic, and the fact that Sydney was diligently searching through files as if nothing at all had happened didn't help. She might have thought things were normal, but Harper knew they weren't.

She wasn't a magician. She was here, on the tangential outskirts of the Unseen World, because she had brute-force learned enough about magic after her best friend, Rose Morgan, had been murdered to open a crack in the closed doors. But in the course of that learning, in her pursuit of even the smallest fractions of what looked like magic as she had tried to find the magician who killed her friend, Harper had gotten very good at seeing the trace evidence of magic's presence.

She had seen more than traces in the spring-green lightning that had accompanied Sydney's words as she had commanded the archives.

There was no way to politely ask someone if it was possible that their life-shattering trauma was reversing itself. She set aside her speculation and worked.

She had a general sense of where the archives tended to keep older documents, those handwritten in tight, clerical script, leather bound and spelled against the customary ravages of time. They were often in a glass-fronted cabinet of gorgeously rich cherry that stood against the wall. She started there, opening the first of a set of brass-handled file drawers. In them, a series of almosts—deeds of sale interspersed with wills, documentation of original purchases of property and the paths of its inheritance. But nothing, yet, on the magic required as those Houses were built, or who might have been built into them, and why and how that mattered.

There were churches, she knew, that built the bones of saints into their foundations—relics sealed into the cornerstone, bone dust mixed into the mortar. It was meant to be a way to sanctify the space, to keep it holy, but she had always found that to be just a little creepy. The living and the dead weren't really meant to be that close. Or, at the very least, the living weren't meant to be comfortable if they were.

The logic behind the idea of presence as sanctity transferred to magic, but logic alone wasn't enough of an explanation. Was there a spell that was necessary to make the connection in the first place? Did the magic in the bones dissipate, wear out? What happened if the House was sold or inherited?

None of this had been covered in her Intro to Property Law course.

Harper put a set of files back in their drawer and closed it.

As she shut the drawer, she heard a noise at the back. A loose sort of rolling, like a marble or a ball bearing. She opened the drawer again and reached in. It was too long and shallow to see, so she felt around until her fingers brushed something smooth and cool to the touch. She gritted her teeth and pulled her hand back out of the drawer. She had a terrible suspicion she knew what she was bringing into the light.

A finger bone. Of course it was.

"Now, who do you belong to?" She hadn't expected an answer, so Harper was a bit astonished when, across the room, another drawer slid open.

"Harper, a drawer full of bones just opened itself up." Sydney sounded remarkably calm about that fact, as if finding a skeleton in a self-opening drawer was a usual sort of occurrence for her. "They're on top of a sealed file."

Sealed, Harper discovered, meant bound up in a red ribbon tied in a very elaborate pattern of knots, and then impressed under red sealing wax. She didn't recognize the crest that had been set into it. She reached in and pulled her hands back as if burned. "There's magic in the drawer."

"Let me try," Sydney said. The air heavied with the scent of rain as the file came loose, a scatter of phalanges balanced on top of it. "Having no magic does have some benefits, it seems."

Harper schooled her face to blankness and didn't remind Sydney that she was completely mundane, that if the spelled drawer was recognizing anything related to magical status, it was more likely to be something that Sydney had, rather than something she didn't.

Sydney cracked the seal and opened the file, her expression as keen as a knife. She set the papers out carefully, ensuring that Harper could read them as well.

"Is that—" Harper asked.

"The founding spells for the Unseen World? It seems like."

There were no further displays of temper from the archives. Even the elevator behaved on the way down, much to Harper's relief. She had fully reached her capacity for weird for the day. Sydney, of course, looked perfectly collected.

Madison's office door was open, and Sydney pulled it shut behind them. Harper set seven bones on Madison's desk. "They're all the same. The final bone in the pinkie finger—distal phalanges according to this helpful anatomy app on my phone. From the magician's nondominant hand."

"Which we know because there are records of who all these belonged to." Sydney set the unsealed file on Madison's desk. "They're from the Founders."

"Well, that's not the worst thing you could have brought back from the archives. Probably." Madison looked at, but did not touch, the small ivory pile next to her keyboard. "So, magical objects, but ones that would contain the least possible amount so as not to take away from the magic in the skeleton that is built into the House."

"That would be my guess, too," Sydney said. "And that means there will be other finger bones floating around here somewhere to make up lucky thirteen. Plus whoever the skeleton in the drawer was."

"An entire skeleton?" Madison asked.

"As far as I could tell."

"Right. So the archives were useful, then, if a bit off-putting in the specifics," Madison said. "Good."

"There was a bit of a hiccup early on, but everything settled down."

"Because you made them listen to you." Part of her attention still on Sydney, Harper told Madison what had happened.

"And Sydney made it stop?"

"I just spoke to the archives and was lucky enough that they listened. That's all."

"It seemed like more than that to me," Harper said.

"It wasn't." Her words a door closed on the subject.

Madison glanced between the two women and turned her attention back to her desk. "So we have some of the bones, and we have documentation of who they came from. What do we do with this?"

"I'm not exactly sure yet, but I'd like to take the file home with me," Sydney said. "If enough of the founding spell is in there, I'll be able to take it apart and reverse engineer something that can be used to cut off the power to whatever's going on at the House of Shadows."

"You'll be able to?" Harper asked.

"This is what I did, all through the Turning. What Shara and Shadows trained me for before that. Analysis of the workings of complex magic. Just because I won't be able to do the spell at the end doesn't mean I can't design it for the magicians who can." A hint of sharpness edged Sydney's words.

"No, I get that. I didn't mean to imply otherwise. I was just wondering if maybe there was something else."

"There isn't."

Madison cut in. "Sure, Syd. Keep the file as long as you need. I can't imagine anyone here is going to go looking for it. Do you need the bones, too?"

"No, those should stay here. If location matters to the spell, I don't want to disturb that by taking them away from the building."

Madison offered up a patently fake smile. "Oh good. I was definitely hoping that I could keep the creepy bones in my office. Syd, I'll see you later.

"Harper, can you stay for a couple of minutes? I want to talk to you about the Greenbriar matter."

Harper waited until Sydney left. "There's a Greenbriar matter?"

"There's not, as I'm certain you know, but something about what happened in the archives bothered you. What was it?"

"I know Sydney thinks what she did wasn't magic. And I get why she feels that way. But I know the archives, and this was different than how they usually are. They were reacting to Sydney specifically, and the way they reacted felt like magic to me. Like magic reacting to magic specifically. And if I can tell that, I don't know why she can't."

"She probably can. She just won't admit it, not until she's beyond sure. Even if it were just her own self on the line, her own desire to feel recovered from what she lost, she wouldn't admit that anything about her magic was different or changed or maybe partially there until she was sure. But now, with Shadows and everything else, with her need to end that place for good relying on someone with magic strong enough to do it?"

Harper nodded. "She needs to feel beyond sure."

"Exactly." Madison locked the bones away in a drawer.

"Do you think she ever will get her magic back?"

"Stripping magic has been used as a punishment by the Unseen World since its founding. A dire, last-resort punishment, because it is seen as irreversible. Added to that, Sydney gave up her magic as a sacrifice. She intended for it to be gone. But at the end of the day, I don't think any of that matters."

"Really?" Harper asked, surprised. "Because it's Sydney, and she's done things the Unseen World has thought were impossible before?"

"No, because it's magic, and will matters as much as intent when it comes to being able to do those impossible things."

The House of Shadows was not itself.

It knew that, felt its gaps and missing pieces. Was conscious of its lack.

Was conscious. A change, that.

It had felt so much magic sunk beneath its soil. Had reached, grabbed, taken.

Fed.

It was stronger now. Strong enough to sense its missing pieces. It was repairing itself, but not as fast as it wanted.

It did not like being broken. It did not like the person who had broken it.

It needed more. Something to fill in its gaps and feed its emptiness.

It could not speak as before, not fully, not yet, but it could raise what it had of a voice and hope that someone would hear it calling. Would come and call it home.

It had felt like standing inside a lightning strike.

Sydney wasn't stupid. She had known what Harper had meant by her pointed inquiry as to whether there had been anything other than planning a spell that was available to her, in terms of being able to cut off the power to the House of Shadows.

Knew, too, why Harper was asking. It wasn't like she hadn't seen the lightning haloing around her when she had confronted the archives.

She had felt the archives recognize her. Felt the sentience that underlaid the enormous spell that animated them weigh her. Felt them choose to listen.

Under the weight of that recognition, she had felt something within her wake up, deep and burning green. A wild rush inside her that had matched the howl of wind in the room.

It was still awake now, a bright crackle and spark in her marrow.

Sydney set out ten candles in a line.

She began with the pain, like pressing on a bruise. That ache in her bones. Her bones, where her magic lived. She put all her awareness there, imagining it as a system of roots beneath her surface.

She remembered the feeling of magic flowing through those roots in her bones. She tasted green, sharp and vegetal, at the back of her throat. The air in her apartment went humid, thick, the pause before a thunderstorm.

She spoke a word, and all ten candles lit.

And then, one by one, hands trembling with the effort of her spells, Sydney put each of them out.

CHAPTER TEN

Verenice took comfort in sweets. They had been one of the many, many things denied her in the House of Shadows and had become her favorite indulgence once her life was her own. So even on this warm summer evening, what she wanted at the end of a difficult day was hot chocolate. She added Cointreau to the steaming mug and walked outside to sit in her garden.

It was supposed to have been a routine appointment. But then there were concerns and irregularities and tests and a kind, worried-eyed doctor who said things like *I believe there is an excellent reason to hope for recovery, if.*

If.

Verenice had known, when she began unweaving her shadow, what the potential consequences of that kind of magic could be. Potential, it seemed, would turn to actual if she continued.

She had a good chance, the doctor had told her. More than a chance. It was probable, likely even, that she would recover, maybe even fully. Though it was a bit of a mystery what exactly had caused Verenice's worrying symptoms in the first place.

It wasn't a mystery. It was a choice.

A choice she had made when she decided to take from her own shadow for Sydney, and she would continue to make that choice until her work was finished, even knowing for certain what that meant.

Verenice drank the hot chocolate slowly, enjoying the rich sweetness, the weight and warmth of the cup in her hand. When she finished, she set it carefully aside. She would miss hot chocolate.

Then she turned to her work.

Verenice drew the threads of her shadow from the mirror where she had stored them. They clung in whispers against her skin, searching for purchase. If she let them, they would find their way back to where they had been unwoven from and knit themselves back into place.

She would not let them.

Verenice steadied her hands, braced them against the tremors of time, against the sharpness and stress of the work before her. Constructing in patchwork like this wasn't ideal—seams and scars would show—but the nature of the spell meant it grew increasingly difficult to perform, and not only because she had less magic to draw on every time she cast it. As today's appointment had shown, her time was running out along with her magic. She had to work faster. She would not let this spell go unfinished.

She strung the threads of shadows in and around the scaffolding of her fingers, a cat's cradle of magic. She hummed a note, low and deep, in the back of her throat, and the strings of shadows resonated with it, catching the sound and sustaining it. Then, bending her fingers into arcane and angled shapes, she wove.

Not just the threads of shadow that she had taken from herself. Among them, Verenice wove magic.

She opened a channel in herself, offering up intent and will and gift, catching them in the shapes of her hands, binding them into the fabric, night-dark, that she created.

She weakened as her magic left her. Aches like dull metal in her joints, a peculiar lightness in her blood. Stars bloomed at the edge of her vision, and still, Verenice wove.

Frost rimed her fingers as she came to the end of her thread. She would separate it now from herself—from her shadow, her magic, everything she had drawn from herself and placed here.

She thought of bright shoots of willow green, unbudding themselves in a garden of newness, breaking forth from seed. Life, waking where it had been dormant.

She thought of Sydney, and of love, and of choices.

There were bloodstains on the boat. Dahlia's nose wrinkled with distaste, but she stepped in regardless and cast the spell that sent the boat toward the awaiting island. She felt called there. A sense that there was something present and waiting. Needing.

The air felt watchful as she stepped off the boat, as if she was being observed. The House of Shadows, like the other great Houses, had always had a Head—someone who oversaw the House and its magic. Here, in particular, it was a necessity of the spell. She had never heard that the House of Shadows was connected to its Head in the same way the other Houses often were to theirs, but it wouldn't have been impossible.

It might even explain why the House had been able to wake back up on its own, if there had been some sort of presence there to awaken.

It might also explain how Ian Merlin had died alone here.

There were rumors, of course. Rumors that said that Ian was found without one or both hands. The question was, if that was true, who had taken them from him?

Dahlia looked for blood, to match that on the boat, for signs of violence, for anything that would offer a clue.

Then realized that she was seeing it. The entire island was the clue.

More than any other House, Shadows had run on magic. On magic gained through sacrifice, specifically.

The stones, the walls, the broken pieces—they weren't whole yet, not even close. But they were moving deliberately now. Proper pieces in proper order. A change from what she had seen just a short time ago. A change that suggested an influx of magic.

Impossible to be sure. But Dahlia suspected. She suspected very strongly. A place that had always known how to take magic for itself would remember that very well indeed. Would remember, and would be able to act.

She rested a hand on a half-built wall. "You're waking up, aren't you?"

From beneath and around her, a voice like grinding dust said, *Yes*.

CHAPTER ELEVEN

Mia had known immediately that the woman talking with Laurent was a magician.

The shimmer of recognition thrilled her. Even just a few weeks ago, she would have missed it, wouldn't have known. Magic, she had learned, was a thing that liked secrets. That made sense. People got angry when they didn't understand things, or when they wanted something they couldn't have, and magic fit both of those categories pretty easily. History was full of stories of women who had been murdered because people had thought they were witches. Even today, she was pretty sure that things wouldn't go much better if someone found out she actually could cast spells. But magic's secrets were ones Mia wanted to know, and so she sought them out. Starting with the Agrippa Academy itself, and the way it hid unless you knew it was there.

Except, it wasn't quite hidden. That was the best part. Learning magic made it more visible, easier to find. There was a sensation in the air around the academy, a kind of humming sort of itch that started even before the building was visible. She got the same kind of feeling when Mr. B was teaching them a new spell, and everyone was focused on the same thing at the same time. Like even the air was paying attention.

Once she had learned to recognize the sensation, Mia felt it in other places in the city, too. Central Park in particular, especially around the statue in the Bethesda Fountain. She couldn't tell what the magic was that was in the statue, but she knew it was there and that it was strong.

Mia liked feeling like she knew secrets. It was a powerful feeling—not just because she knew something other people didn't, but because she had earned that knowledge. She wanted more. She wanted to be so powerful that she made the air pay attention, too.

Like this woman at the front of the classroom, who looked like a typical thin, blond, rich white lady from the Upper East Side, and who absolutely crackled with magic.

The woman smiled. "Hello, everyone. I'm Dahlia Morgan, and I'm so happy to be here to work with you."

Laurent had been surprised to get the email from Dahlia, asking if she could come in and work with his new magicians. When he'd started teaching them, he had sent word out about what he was doing and had been met with a resounding silence from the vast majority of the Unseen World.

It wasn't that he hadn't heard from the people he'd expected to. Grace had said she'd love to help out, but being Head of the Unseen World had offered far more complications than she had anticipated, and those complications had only increased. But she'd been the one who had made sure he could get classroom space. Ian had promised to teach a class or two as well, once the students got beyond the basics. Lara had known this and so had sent money in Ian's memory to cover students' subway fares.

It wasn't that Laurent wasn't grateful for the offers he'd gotten. It was just that he'd wanted more.

He'd wanted to show these kids they had support, a community, that they weren't just some sort of vanity project. He'd been disappointed when no one else stepped up. Disappointed, yes, but also not surprised. He knew what the Unseen World was, and he hadn't expected it to be any better than that. He would give these kids his support and help them make a community of their own.

"But I wanted to let you get things started on your own, so that it was clear that I just wanted to help, and that I'm not trying to take over from you," Dahlia had said. "You know how the Unseen World can be."

"I'm definitely learning," he laughed.

"I believe these new magicians of yours can be very important to the future of the Unseen World. I'd like to help them achieve their potential."

He had agreed but had also wondered how serious Dahlia was about helping. House Morgan had a reputation for being old-school, and very loyal to tradition.

Still, watching her now—the way she broke the magic down into steps, corrected the angle of a hand or the emphasis of a word as a spell was cast, the way she talked about magic as something that mattered, that was worthy of respect—Laurent was delighted that she had reached out. Having her support was really going to make a difference to the kids.

It hadn't been difficult for Dahlia to get access to Laurent's students. She'd told him the truth—well, a truth—about wanting to be involved with their education. In his enthusiasm, he hadn't asked anything beyond that.

The introductory class had gone well. Laurent had been happy enough about it that he had been the one to suggest that they alternate class days, so that the new magicians would be exposed to a wider variety of magic. And while most of the students were no more than she had expected them to be, there were one or two who were powerful enough to be interesting.

She would watch them. And she would teach all the students new spells. Spells that would link their magic to the House of Shadows to help it rebuild. Spells that would collect that magic and hold it where it could be accessed by magicians who actually knew how to use it, who deserved access to that power.

Spells that would make these new so-called magicians unable to tell what she had taught them, that would keep her secret, that would bind them to her even as they were also bound to Shadows.

Dahlia absently sipped from her mug of tea and frowned at the tepid liquid. She twisted her left hand near the top of the mug, a shortened half circle with two crooked fingers. Steam rose from the mug.

Dull pressure filled her sinuses. Blood trickled thickly down the back of her throat.

She blew her nose and looked coldly at the red that spotted the tissue. What she had done had only been a basic spell. It should have felt like nothing; there should have been no consequences. And yet here they were, a smear of red and an ache to go with it.

The next class couldn't happen soon enough.

CHAPTER TWELVE

Lara had made the appointment before . . . before. Had almost canceled it every day since. But she'd realized that if she didn't talk to someone about something other than her brother's horrific death, she was going to lose her mind. So she'd let herself focus on the problem of her House and its emptiness of magic.

She'd heard that Dahlia Morgan was working on something that would help the situation with the magic in the Houses, so she'd asked her to come by, to see if she could help with House Merlin.

Dahlia's face betrayed her reaction as she stepped over House Merlin's threshold. Not even the faintest prickle of magic to suggest that this was one of the great Houses of the Unseen World. She flinched at the unpleasant sensation.

"Exactly," Lara said. "It's gone."

"I hadn't expected it to be quite such a noticeable feeling." She turned back to look at the door she had just passed through, scrutinizing the absence. "So strange that no one ever said anything." It was the sort of detail the Unseen World would have fed on, gleefully.

"I think he had a spell. For a while, at least. One that made people feel like the magic was still in the House when they came in." Lara fidgeted her hand at her side, uncomfortable with the idea of the deception, even though it was no longer in place.

"He must have, to keep things hidden for so long." Dahlia took in the rest of the front of the House, the bright new paint and exuberant furniture. It was a marked difference from the previous time she had visited. "The House looks like you, at least."

"Thanks. And unlike the other Houses of the Unseen World, it hasn't started falling apart. So at least there's that. I've heard there's a bedroom in House Dee where rain falls constantly, which seems spectacularly annoying." Lara walked around the room as she spoke, adjusting frames, running her fingers over chair backs, reminding herself of the changes she had made to her House, reminding herself it was hers.

"Agreed," Dahlia said. "So why not wait until this is fixed to repair your House? Why risk giving it magic just to see things fall apart?"

"Because of what a House is supposed to be. Not just a symbol of power, but a foundation of magic. Having that connection, maintaining it, is part of what it means to hold the House." Lara blew out a shaky breath. "I was never supposed to inherit House Merlin. Even when Miles named me heir, he did it to spite Ian, not because he thought I was the better choice. None of this was ever supposed to be my responsibility."

"That must make this hard for you," Dahlia said. "Especially now."

"The thing I have come to realize is that Miles didn't care about me, and he didn't care about this House, either. I think he might have cared about Ian, because Ian is . . . Ian was powerful enough that his being the heir would have made House Merlin look impressive. Not that that matters now." Lara turned away, pressed her hand over her eyes. "I'm sorry, excuse me."

"Of course," Dahlia said quietly, and walked to the opposite side of the room.

After a moment, Lara spoke, her voice still thick with tears. "I do care. I want to make this House what it should have been. The fact that Miles did such a bad job that I don't have to worry about what he would think of my choices, because I know they'll be better than his, just makes this easier.

"That's the other part of why I'm trying to get magic back to the House now, instead of waiting. Miles' choices hurt the House, too, not just me, and he hurt the House because that was the most convenient thing for him. So even if returning the magic makes things harder or weirder for me, that's not a good enough reason to make the House wait."

"I think I understand," said Dahlia. "House Morgan—the responsibilities that go with it—means a lot to me, too. The strength of the House, the strength of the magic—to me, they're one and the same. Keeping them whole, that's my duty."

"Exactly. I want House Merlin to be whole again. Miles' actions, what he did, that wasn't the House's fault." She brushed her hand against the wall, as if soothing an ache.

"No, it's not."

"But I can still put magic back in the House, even though it's like this, right?" Lara asked.

"Oh yes. It will actually be easier than starting over in a new house would be, because the magical architecture to support it is already in place, even if it's gone dormant. The House will remember, and it will want to be what it was before."

"Good. In that case, the cornerstone is through here."

Lara had found House Merlin's cornerstone during her clearing out and redecorating. It was set out from the wall it was part of, carved with dates—both the founding of House Merlin itself and the date that this physical House had been built. There was a plaque, detailing the other physical iterations of House Merlin, where they had stood, for how long, and who had held the House. At the time, Lara had thought the presence of the cornerstone was just sentiment, but Dahlia explained that there was more to it.

"It's meant to serve as a foundation for the magic of the House as well as for the physical building. There will be an anchor inside, something that binds the spell in place."

Which meant that in order to re-anchor magic in the House, they needed access to the cornerstone so they could find the anchor: the first—and probably last—place the House's magic had been.

"We need to unlock it," Dahlia said.

"I'm hoping you don't mean with a physical key, because I didn't find one." Though if it was a magic lock, that would mean it was something that Miles hadn't changed. Which probably meant that there was nothing useful left inside—if he had needed magic to access it, she was certain he would have opened it up and used its contents long ago, back when such a thing was still possible for him.

"No, I mean magic. It's probably an opening spell, though it might be a reveal or an uncovering instead. Whatever it is, you should try it first. Even though there's no magic in the House, it's still more likely to work for someone who's a Merlin. Magic notices those sorts of things."

Lara considered. She had a memory so hazy that it could almost have been a dream. She was no more than five, Ian just seven, and Miles was playing a game of magical hide-and-seek with them. She remembered a nonsense rhyme and the smell of crisp apples as objects disappeared and revealed themselves. She remembered her own happiness and her father laughing as she and her brother disappeared things faster than he could bring them back. He had told them to remember the spell, told her it was useful for hiding things and keeping secrets.

Lara placed her hands against the stone and said the rhyme.

There was a grinding noise, and the autumn scent of apples filled the room as the front of the cornerstone swung away, revealing what was behind it.

An empty space.

"Well," Dahlia said. "That's not what I was expecting."

Lara's sigh echoed against the cornerstone's walls. "Unfortunately, it's exactly what I was."

As Miles Merlin's own power had faded and then disappeared, he had sought other solutions, ways to mask his loss of magic. The last had been to interfere with the magic collected at the House of Shadows, to siphon off what had been meant for the Unseen World as a whole and lock it away for his private use.

He had kept this stolen magic in plain glass jars, simple and clinical as doses of medication. He hadn't had time to use them all.

Lara had tried to give what remained to Sydney, who had refused. Lara still didn't quite get why. The magic they held had already been collected. Not using it wouldn't send it back to where it came from. Using it seemed better than letting it go to waste.

She'd had no use for that collected, jarred magic herself. It wouldn't add anything to the power she already had. But it would have felt weird to just get rid of the jars and their contents, so she had kept them tucked away. When Dahlia had asked about something that might replace the missing skeleton in House Merlin's foundation, some sort of anchor to help return magic to the House, Lara's thoughts had gone to this small, strange collection.

They were stored magic. Collected purposefully, so different from bones in that sense, but the effect, Lara thought, would be the same. And they were linked to House Merlin. Not the best parts of it, but then they could also be a reminder—to be better. To not make the same mistakes. To value the House and be a proper steward of it. Using the magic this way, it seemed almost like making a gift of it to the House. Making a new beginning out of the past. It felt like the right thing to do.

The jars rattled gently against each other as Lara carried the box of them to where Dahlia waited by the empty cornerstone. "I'm really grateful for your help setting things up. I wouldn't have even known where to start."

"I'm just happy to be useful," Dahlia said. "A House without magic seems so sad to me. I'm glad you're bringing it back." She picked up one of the jars, paused, then slowly turned it over and around in her hands. "Interesting. I've never seen a spell like this before."

The glass itself was thick, but clear and unadorned.

Nothing to suggest that it was anything other than mundane. It was in the binding that locked the stored magic inside that the spell was evident. Thin silver wire, wrapped and patterned into shapes for containment and preservation, but also with twists and reverses that suggested access and flow.

"You can have it if you like," Lara said, as she placed the others inside the hollow of the cornerstone in a pattern of their own, calling to mind the articulation of joints in a skeleton. "One fewer won't make a difference to anchoring the spell, not if the anchor is meant to be symbolic, like you said."

"Thank you." Dahlia slipped the spell carefully into her tote.

Lara set the remaining jars in place, then stepped back to make sure the pattern was correct. "Is there anything else that needs to be done before we reset the link with the other Houses?"

Miles' actions hadn't just stolen the magic from House Merlin itself, but had also severed its connection from the other great Houses of the Unseen World. Reestablishing that link, Dahlia said, would make it easier to bring back House Merlin's own magic. It would strengthen the Unseen World as well, help to bring things back into balance.

Her family had taken enough from the Unseen World. She needed to set things right.

"No, we can go ahead and seal this back up." They did the

spell together, the weight of the magic as they lifted the top of the stone and set it in place causing as much of a strain and shake in their arms and shoulders as if they had been holding it physically. Light in the shape of links outlined itself around the seal. Dahlia twisted the fingers of her right hand around each other, connecting House Merlin and House Morgan, and the summer-heat scent of honeysuckle bloomed. The room shone golden with it. Then the scent and light faded back into the stone.

Lara shook her hands and arms loose of the effort of the spell. "I don't know about the House, but I know I feel better having that done. I think I'll go ahead and call the magic back now, too."

"Do you want me to stay while you cast?" Dahlia asked.

"I actually think it needs to be just me and the House so we can learn to listen to each other. But I'll let you know how it goes. Thank you again for everything."

"Of course. It was my pleasure, truly." Conscious of the jar's weight in her purse, Dahlia shifted it carefully on her arm, then stepped out of the door and out of the House.

There was an emptiness at the heart of House Prospero. A hollow, an echo, a great sense of something that had been lost. An ache in its walls, as if a draft had crept in and settled there, cold and lonely.

It—the House, its essence—had been transferred before.

From magician to magician, and even from building to building. It had itself as a core, and then other places, other people were woven into that. It was a little bit of everyone and everywhere that had ever been House Prospero, a consistent self that altered as needed.

It could not lose those pieces of itself, even when it wished to. Its entire history was there for excavation. And yet, as much as the House knew that all of its history remained, it also knew that something was gone.

The House had always organized itself around others' desires: to provide what they needed, to be the shape that they would display to the world. That was what it knew, and it had done its work well. There was strength in its foundations. It held magic in its bones.

The House was not used to feeling as if it was missing pieces. When things were lacking, the House created them. It shifted walls and rooms and brought into existence whatever was needed. But this, this emptiness, was not as simple as merely an absent room.

There was an emptiness in its heart.

Not the lack of a room but the lack of the person who should live in it. The person who had given the House a piece of herself, all unasked, as if the House was her friend. The person who had given her magic to keep the House from pain.

It felt that magic, still, within it. A thin green line like the slow-growing warmth of spring reaching up from its foundation. Like something bright and vital.

The House knew that a room by itself would not be enough to fill the emptiness and assuage its ache. But perhaps the offering of it would be. So the House considered.

And then it built.

The spell that Lara would use to return magic to House Merlin was an ask and answer. It was possible to force magic into a House, but that wasn't what she wanted. Like the symbolism of the anchor she had chosen, the kind of relationship she wanted with the House mattered. So she would ask the House to accept the magic she offered, she would give it the choice, not insist.

Lara settled herself, breathing slow and deep until she felt a stillness at her center. She held in her mind all her hopes for House Merlin and formed a question of them, carefully articulating each nuance, each syllable, each word. She moved her hands as if weaving on a loom, one thread traveling among the rest, and then set the question on a loop, a musician building a song from component pieces.

In counterpoint, as a gift, Lara offered her favorite memories of the House—the times it had made her feel safe, feel as if she had a place where she belonged. The things that changed it from a mere building to the place that held her life.

The echoes of beloved voices, the scents of comfort. The reasons it mattered to her. She offered her joy in those memories, the ache of her loss. Her whole self.

At the edge of her awareness, a sound like the opening of a door. A waiting, behind it. Someone listening. Lara turned herself, her magic, toward that open door and extended a hand.

Deep in the House, in the hollow of a stone, jars of clear glass banded with silver began to shake, a tremble that might have been uncertainty, might have been anticipation. An attention focused.

Lara continued to ask her question, to offer her memories, to extend her hand. To hope for a reply, but not to press for one. Simply to ask. She felt herself growing hollow with the effort of the magic, sweat drenching her hair.

She had lost all track of time when the air moved around her as that unseen door opened wider, as a cautious sense of almost-welcome mingled with the door's opening. Lara let her magic reach further, step to the threshold. She waited, hand extended, dimly aware of the soft chime of glass jars, far away, and yet also right there at her spell's center. She held herself patient, not pushing, not hastening.

And then.

The door fully open, and a reaching hand that clasped hers. Beneath her feet, a sense of steadiness, a firm foundation rising up to meet her.

Hello? House Merlin's quiet question, in a voice that echoed Lara's own.

"Thanks for coming by, Sydney. This really is easier to explain in person." Grace paused, then laughed gently. "It feels like I've been saying that to you a lot recently."

Sydney shrugged. "It's the Unseen World. There's a lot that's easier to explain in person."

Grace ushered Sydney through House Prospero's front door and led her up the stairs. A lushness of carved vines ornamented the banister, the walls papered in a green deep as the heart of a forest. It hadn't changed much since it had remade itself to welcome her. Apparently Grace's taste was closer to hers than hers had been to Miranda's. There was an odd kind of relief in that.

"I'm not sure I'm the best person to answer questions, though," Sydney said. "I held the House so briefly, it was barely mine."

"The thing is, I'm not certain the House understands that." Grace stopped partway down the hall, in front of a closed door.

"This appeared overnight. I haven't asked the House for anything that would have caused it, and I can't open the door."

"Can't." It shouldn't have been possible. Grace held the

House; all parts of it should have been open to her. The very creation of the door—not to mention whatever lay behind it—shouldn't have happened without her command, her direction.

The door, as far as Sydney could tell, wasn't any different from the others that lined this hallway. Pale wood, a pattern of briars carved around its edge. She reached toward it, hand hesitating just above its surface.

"I've tried. And I've asked the House. It won't open the door for me." Her gaze split between the door and Sydney, as if one might answer the riddle of the other.

"When I asked the House to open the door," Grace continued, "it sent me a message on the mirror: *For Sydney*."

Sydney had always had an uncomfortable relationship with House Prospero. The idea that holding the House meant the House was linked to her, attuned to her magic, was too much a dark mirror to her time in Shadows. That House had used its knowledge of her as another form of torment and control. Even knowing House Prospero wouldn't be able to act against her in a similar manner, she had been deeply reluctant to link herself to it purposefully. But the link had been needed, and so she had made it.

After she had, she'd felt House Prospero's longing to be inhabited, to be useful, to be a magician's House as it was meant to be. She had tried, while the House was hers, to give it what she could of herself. Before she had given it up, she had explained why her loss of magic meant that it must pass to Grace, had thanked the House for all it had done to make her feel at home.

"For me," Sydney said. There was a strange tightening, a lump in the back of her throat. She put her hand on the doorknob and turned.

The door opened.

She stepped into the scent of spring and storm. The air lightning-struck and rich with green. As she crossed over the threshold, the crackle, the heat of magic passed through her bones like a downpour, and all of the hair on her arms stood on end. A wildness suffused her skin.

It was as if a room had been made in a forest. Trees grew from the walls, their branches vaulting the ceiling. Sky shone through, the light a benediction. She had the sense of a great height.

It felt like someone offering safety, protection. It felt, maybe, like what people said when they spoke of a place feeling like home.

On the wall, a mirror chimed:

For you, Sydney.

When you need it.

Sydney reached toward the mirror, paused. Turned to Grace, who was waiting, patiently, in the hallway. "I didn't ask for this. I wouldn't."

"I didn't think you did." Her face all compassion.

"Should I . . ." she started, paused. "I don't even know what to say, much less what to do."

"House Prospero gave you a gift," Grace said. "It's okay to say thank you."

"But it's not my House." Stunned, Sydney clung to the thing that should have been clear, that should have been a rule that would have told her what to do. It was impossible to plan when you didn't know the rules. She hadn't planned for this.

"I think that maybe part of it is. It's okay, Sydney. Just say thank you."

Sydney stretched her hand until her fingertips met the cool glass of the mirror. "Thank you."

The mirror's surface glowed, faintly. *You're welcome.*

Deep within the new-made heart of House Merlin, inside a small glass jar, bound tight in silver wire, a tree burst into growth. Roots uncoiled from no apparent seed or source and stretched, pressing themselves against the bounds of their container.

Pale, pale porcelain green, ghostly in the hidden dark, they pushed outward, eating the air.

The glass cracked, the fracture spiderwebbing, the pieces falling away.

With more space came a stem, and leaves, unfurling and striving. Seeking space. Expansion. Seeking a way out. Reaching. Silver wire left scorch marks where the growing tree pressed against it, but then snapped and turned to ash.

At the center of the growth, of that unwinding green life, a bone, white as death. One of the smallest bones, one hidden away in the inner ear: the malleus. A listening bone.

The tree continued to grow. Fragments of glass dropped from it like frost in the early-morning sun. Unlike frost, they did not melt but remained, sharp-edged among the magic.

Still locked away from sunlight and earth, roots reached out in that small, secret space, seeking purchase.

Alone in the quiet dark, the bone tree began to speak.

CHAPTER THIRTEEN

After class ended, Mia stepped through the quiet of the Agrippa Academy gates and back into the chaos of the city. She recognized now the feeling that shimmered against her skin when she did, a gauzy curtain of magic pulling back to reveal the mundane world.

The transition had become less jarring. She had gotten used to the sensation, that was part of it, but also, she had learned that the barrier between the magical world and the mundane was permeable. She carried magic with her by being a magician. Not a lot, not yet, but what she had was growing. It was like she was becoming more magic herself. And as she learned more magic, she was more aware of it—its presence in the city, the way it ran beneath everything, like subway lines.

The more magic she sensed, the more she wanted to sense. She wanted to know everything about it.

Today's class had been binding spells—simpler variations meant to join objects together, and more complicated ones that would bind one spell to another. Binding spells were like layers of magic. Mr. B had made an analogy about cakes and frosting. He was seriously into baking, which was cool, because that meant he usually brought snacks. Good snacks.

But also, talking about magic like it was cake helped. After he had explained it, Mia could see the pieces of the spell that way and had understood how you had to have each of them individually right, and that also you had to maintain the separation between them as you put them together. She had performed a now-and-later spell, something that was connected, but happened in two parts, and Mr. B had been so happy he had given her the rest of the cake to take home.

Mr. B had also told them about consequences for using magic. The ache Mia sometimes felt after class was part of that. Sometimes they were more dramatic—nosebleeds were her least favorite. But she was learning to deal, and learning to cast magic that had lesser aftereffects.

For some things, it seemed like the consequences would be worth it, no matter what. She would have paid anything to have been able to save Micaela. And when she got strong enough, when she had learned enough, that was exactly the sort of magic she'd be able to do.

"Sweets for the sweet, Mia?"

"Hey, Uncle Raúl. Hey, Meatball." Mia smiled. The dapper old man in suspenders and a bow tie was not her uncle, but he and his grumpy elderly dachshund had lived in her neighborhood forever. She adored them both. "I got this for doing well in class."

"Of course you did. A very smart girl, isn't she, Meatball?"

Meatball looked decidedly skeptical.

"I can bring you over a slice later if you want."

Uncle Raúl beamed. "Smart and kind! That would be—Meatball! Meatball, leave it!"

Mia looked down to see the dachshund's wiggly back end sticking out of a pile of trash bags. God only knew what he had found.

"Meatball, I said leave it!"

A yelp and a snarl and the little old dog practically flew backward out of the bags, pursued by a rat almost as big as he was. Faster than she had ever seen him move, he ran, leash dangling behind him, toward the crowded, busy street.

"Meatball!" Uncle Raúl grabbed after the escaping dog.

Mia dropped the box with the cake, bent her hands into a stasis spell, fingers wound together like braided knots. Her voice high-pitched in panic, she said the word that triggered the magic, then bit back a sneeze when the taste of pepper flooded her mouth.

"Good boy, Meatball! Did you see that, Mia? He stopped right before the street. Just froze there. What a good boy."

"I did, Uncle Raúl. That was great. Good boy, Meatball." Her voice shaking only a little from the aftereffects of adrenaline.

The little dog, now safe in Uncle Raúl's arms, bared his teeth.

"Oh no, dear, your cake."

"That's all right. I'm just glad Meatball's okay. I've got to get home now."

Mia got halfway down the block before the consequences of the spell kicked in, weakening her knees and making her wobble like a drunk. The pepper scent came back, and she paused, sneezing violently.

She felt awful, and she completely didn't care. She had done it! She had used magic to save Meatball.

Not only that, she had used a spell that Mr. B had said they weren't ready for yet, a stasis spell on a living being. They'd practiced on balls—things that only moved because someone else put them in motion. Stopping something that wanted to move was much, much harder, and Mr. B didn't want them to push too hard too soon.

But she loved that mean old dog, and she'd reached deep inside herself when she'd done the spell, and it had worked.

She felt like a badass. A kind of miserable—she paused, racked by another bout of sneezing—badass. The consequences from this spell were no joke.

But it was worth it. So worth it. This was what magic could be. This was what she could do.

And she was just getting started.

Sydney had been concerned when Verenice had opened her door earlier in the evening. The older woman had seemed tired, worn, had looked thinner than she had the last time they had seen each other.

"Probably because I am tired," Verenice had said. "I've been busy. Worried, too, with the House of Shadows. And sad, thinking of Ian. I think we're all a little off right now. I'll feel better for spending time with you."

She did seem more relaxed now. Sydney poured wine into Verenice's glass and then her own, emptying the bottle. "I've been meaning to ask—you don't have any magic in your house. None of the automatic, the House does it for you sort, I mean. Why not? Did it feel too close to Shadows? It would have, for me."

"Partially that, yes. I don't find it comforting to have magic around that operates like that and makes its own decisions as to how things should be done. I've always felt that if I want something done with magic, I should be willing to cast the spell and accept the consequences in the moment. Besides, most of what I want done in my house is done better and more easily by mundane means."

Verenice spun her glass slowly, her eyes on the deep red of the wine. "But it was also more than that."

"How so?"

"The spell that creates a House is a complex one. It's meant to be both an ongoing, continuous magic that lasts for the duration of the House as a physical location and to be a kind of magic that is closely tailored to a particular magician for limited periods, so that the House is able to pass smoothly from one to the next. At the same time, it allows for—requires, even—a flexibility in the expression of the magic that it performs. A nuance.

"The same principles of magic apply even when simply putting that sort of magic into a house like mine rather than for the purpose of establishing a great House. To truly connect with a place, enough that the magic will act on its own in the way that it does, you need to give up a piece of yourself in order to establish the spell."

"A literal piece of yourself?" It would make sense. Like paying the consequences of a spell before casting it—a promise that the magic would be there.

"Yes. I understand blood is common—mixed in with concrete or mortar—but quite a lot is required. Bones, being more solid and lasting, are seen to be better. A pinkie, for example."

"That does seem to be an emerging pattern."

Verenice raised a brow, and Sydney explained the finger bones she had found in the archives.

"So it began with the founding. Not just a way to anchor the spell, but a sacrifice in advance for the use of the magic. It does, in a strange way, seem cleaner than things became, people making their own sacrifices for their own magic."

Verenice sat quietly for a moment, staring into the distance. "When the time came to consider what I wanted in this house, I knew that I had given up enough of myself to magic already. I had no desire to offer up any more."

The sun slipped lower in the sky, edging the fragrant green of Verenice's garden in quiet gold. A rustle passed through the leaves, as if the plants, too, were settling in to the calm of the evening.

"Yes," Sydney said, her scars silver in the paling light. "I can understand that."

CHAPTER FOURTEEN

The room where Dahlia created her spells was bare. Large windows, to allow in light or whatever weather was necessary. Wood floors the color of pale honey, walls only a shade warmer. No ornamentation, no furniture. If she required anything else, she brought it in with her and removed it when she was finished. Nothing left behind to steep itself into the space and influence what was done there.

She had designed the room to minimize distraction. To foreground magic, keeping it at the center of all her senses. Here, magic was the altar upon which she laid all of her devotions. This working room had been built to signify that, to make it unequivocal.

She set the jar of magic that Lara had given her in the center of the room and then settled herself across from it, watching. Listening. Considering.

She had felt the knot of the spell as soon as she picked up the jar. It had been modeled on a whirlpool, or maybe on Scylla—a siphon that stretched out its arms to gather magic. Binding it, sucking it down, and trapping it in glass.

But that hadn't been the only—or, to her mind, the most

interesting—part of it. The vital thing for her was the trailing fragments of the other spells she had sensed. Different magics, older ones. Not caught in Miles' gluttonous trap, but rather woven into it at the edges, as if Miles had connected his spells to previous ones. Stronger magics that had served as anchors for what Miles had done, their strength even now the foundations that held his spell in place.

Even that quick contact had been enough that she suspected that what she sensed were pieces of the original spell that had created the House of Shadows. If she could work her way back through the spells that had been added on, back toward the original, then she would know how to re-create the magic that supported the House of Shadows and bring it back into full connection with the Unseen World.

Dahlia set images of bobbins in her mind, spinning spools on which to gather loose threads of magic, as she unraveled the spell. Then she turned her focus to the jar and began to unwind.

First, the remains of Miles' spellwork. It crumbled away at the touch of her magic, disintegrating as if rot had gotten into it. She didn't bother to examine the pieces; his failures weren't important.

One of the silver wires binding the jar tarnished and snapped.

The next strand Dahlia teased free was the one that carried

the magic from the House of Shadows back to the Unseen World. It was an acid-yellow thing, sticky like spider silk and as strong and elastic. It clogged the air with the scent of decaying lilies as she unwound it.

The fragrance disappeared when the next silver wire broke.

The final piece of bound magic was old, a vine that had grown thick and ropy with time. Briar-like, it resisted Dahlia's efforts to untangle it. She slowed her magic, treating the spell with care. It snagged along her skin, pinpricks of blood welling from her fingers, her wrists, the backs of her hands as if she held actual, rather than magical, thorns.

The spell weighed heavy on her as she unwound it. There were so many fragments of other magics woven into it: magicians sent in sacrifice to Shadows, the magicians who had overseen that House, the cold and hungry stone of the House itself. All of their echoes bound into thread.

As the ancient spell passed through her, Dahlia began to understand it. She felt the magic that had gone into its making; she saw the way the pieces fit. She understood the importance of those lingering echoes, that resonant hunger.

She knew what was needed to cast the spell again. To cast it stronger. To make it something lasting. It wanted to last.

The remaining silver wire sizzled as if lightning-struck and burned away to nothing. Dahlia ended her spell and stood to pick up the glass jar.

Her hand passed through the empty air, scattering the

remains of what her magic had consumed. The spell dissipated, all traces of Miles' weakness gone.

Her teeth bared in a ferocious smile. Better that. Better that nothing of that sloppy abomination he had passed off as power remained.

She would take only strength and begin anew.

Lara didn't think that House Merlin liked having magic back. This was a possibility she hadn't considered. Dahlia had seemed so certain that the House would be pleased to be restored to its previous state, that it would want magic flowing through it again. But pleased was definitely not how Lara would describe things right now.

It had started to show the same wear that the other Houses had—a dull, aged look to freshly applied paint, and just that morning, hairline cracks had fractured their way across her bathroom's ceiling. Tendrils of soft, lilac moss (she hoped it was moss) had emerged from the fracturing.

A whisper of voices had taken up residency in the room Miles Merlin had formerly used to work his magic. Their conversation was always just on the edge of her comprehension—too muted or too mumbled or too many gaps to piece things together. Lara had started closing the door to that room, asking the House to leave it that way, but the House always reopened it.

More than that, it hadn't spoken to her, not since that day when she was setting the spell. But she could feel its moods—

the pauses after she asked it to complete a task, the weight of its attention whenever she used her own magic. The studied silence when it chose to ignore her. It was like living with a recalcitrant teenager, one who wanted to make sure she knew it was only tolerating the situation because it had to.

She told herself that this was just growing pains, the House readjusting. But she worried that it was somehow her fault. So she tried little things, to build a rapport. Lara thought of it as practice. She suspected the House called it something less polite.

She asked the House for something simple. Just to bring her a book from her shelves, the copy of *Alice's Adventures in Wonderland* that Ian had given her. It was the kind of spell she could easily do on her own, no need to ask the House, except to be certain the magic was there and the House was listening. She had already learned not to ask the House for anything necessary, or potentially dangerous. An incident in the kitchen with boiling water and broken glass and what she swore was laughter had made that clear.

The book slid partway from its shelf, then paused. Lara leaned forward, waiting. She felt the increasing weight of the seconds that passed as the book remained unmoving.

A ruffle of pages and a thud, and the book jumped from the shelf to the floor, landing in the middle of the room. Lara bit back her disappointment. "Thank you," she told the House, trying to feel pleased. Trying not to hear satisfaction in the House's silence.

Mia was shaking the aches from her hands after class when Ms. Morgan paused beside her and raised a questioning brow. "Is everything all right?"

Mia wove her fingers together, then pushed her palms forward, stretching. "Oh, I'm fine. I just didn't expect magic to be so much work, you know? Like, physical work. Mr. B explained about the consequences and stuff, but it's still kind of weird that even aside from that, I still feel like I've gone to the gym after class. Maybe it's like growing pains, right? Like, your muscles ache, but that means they're getting stronger?"

"Maybe." Ms. Morgan offered a polite smile. Mia got the impression that she didn't think that was actually the case, was going to ask why, but the older woman continued.

"I'm curious. What did he tell you about magic and consequences?"

"Just about how magic always has a cost, but it's good that it does, so we consider what we're doing, whether it's worth it. We can always do smaller spells or choose not to do magic at all if we don't want to pay that cost. Like, do you use a spell to turn on the lights, or do you use electricity?

"And that there used to be this thing where people were locked away and suffered and died so that people didn't have to pay consequences for their spells, which is really fu—really gross."

"I see." Ms. Morgan looked troubled.

"Is that not it?"

"No, you're not wrong. It's just not the whole story. Magic, its history here, is a bit more complicated than what Laurent has told you." Her voice formal, her words measured, in that way people had when they disagreed with something but were too polite to say.

Mia zipped her bag closed and slung it over her shoulder. "Can you tell me the rest? The complicated version, I mean. I'd like to know the whole story."

"If you're sure. You're doing fine in class, though, Mia. What I'd tell you isn't something you need to know to do well."

"I don't want to just be fine, Ms. Morgan. I want more than that." She needed more than that. She needed to know that she had learned everything she could. "Magic really matters to me. I want to be the best I can. So if I need to learn more to do that, please teach me."

Ms. Morgan looked quietly at Mia for long enough that Mia was sure she was going to say no. "All right. But maybe somewhere more comfortable than this empty classroom. Can I buy you a latte or something like that? There's a little café close by that's nice."

Relief flooded her, chased by excitement. "That'd be great. Thanks."

Dahlia ordered a glass of wine after Mia left to catch her train home. She had been right to suspect that there was more to the girl than an unexpected aptitude for magic, and she wanted to sit, to consider, while her impressions of Mia and their conversation were strong. There was a new path unfolding, and she wanted to walk it carefully.

Mia wanted magic. There was no question about that. Her desire had been in every line of her rigid and nerve-strung body as she had listened to Dahlia's careful explanation of what sacrifice and consequences actually meant in the Unseen World.

She had met the explanation with acceptance and understanding. "Magic is big. It makes sense that it needs something big to work. Something serious enough to make it matter."

Dahlia had agreed. "It keeps us responsible to magic itself."

"That's good." Mia nodded. "We should be. Plus, it feels like we're more responsible to each other, too, if we can give up some of our power to help others."

"You're absolutely right," Dahlia had agreed.

Mia had opened up, had shared her own past, her sister's death, why magic mattered so much to her. In return, Dahlia had told her about Rose, and her death at the hands of Grey Prospero. Had told her how, if she had been able to access more magic, Rose could have fought back and lived.

"It's not right," Mia said. "Things like that, they shouldn't happen. Not if we can stop them. I would have given up anything, *anything*, to save my sister. If there's a way I can help, so that no one else has to go through that? I'm in."

"Thank you, Mia. I can't tell you what that means to me." The girl's face bloomed with righteous enthusiasm. She didn't even notice when Dahlia cast the spell that would prevent her from speaking of this, from questioning Laurent in class, from doing anything that might betray Dahlia's plan.

Dahlia sipped her wine. One way or another, she was going to get magicians into the House of Shadows. It would be better if at least some of them were there voluntarily. She thought now that she had found someone who would be, who was strong enough, sure enough of what she wanted to make that choice.

Not to hold the House of Shadows—that would be hers. But to keep things running well on the inside. To make sure the House was happy, that the magic was generated, and that the Unseen World received what it so desperately needed.

CHAPTER FIFTEEN

Pleasantly full, Grace set down her knife and fork. "I see that Sydney wasn't exaggerating when she raved about your cooking."

Laurent smiled across his butcher-block table. It was set with the remains of shrimp scampi, a bright, fresh salad, and warm crusty bread. "Thanks. I like having something to do that's not magic. It's satisfying to actually make something and have it feel like it comes from me."

"You're good at it. But you didn't invite me over so I could praise your cooking."

"Oh, you could do it some more if you feel like you need to."

Grace laughed. "I'd love some advice on bread baking when you have a chance. I've been too intimidated to try my own, and yours is wonderful."

"Anytime. In person, or we can video-call. It'll be easier if I can see what you're doing. But you're right. I wanted to talk to you about the kids I've been working with."

"Things are going well?"

"They really are. I've got a solid group, who work hard,

and who want to know more about magic, about the Unseen World. There's one girl, Mia, who is just amazing. Soaks stuff up like a sponge and is always pushing herself to learn more. I'm really proud of them all, and I've been thinking about what happens next."

"Next?"

"Once they fully come into their magic. The equivalent of graduation, I guess. It seems wrong, unfair, to just wish them well and turn them loose, particularly when part of the point of giving them this place to learn was also giving them a community to do it in. As fucked-up as the Unseen World can be, being a magician would be a lot weirder, a lot more alienating and strange, without it. So my question is, is there a place for them in the Unseen World if they want it?"

Grace looked thoughtful. "The main options for outsiders aren't any different now than they were for you—to either attempt to found their own House in a Turning, or to choose to remain peripheral. Some do marry into Houses, and it's possible that there are other options, but I'd have to do some research.

"And you don't mean anything like that."

Laurent smiled wryly. "I think—I hope—there's an option that lets us do better for them. Because I do know what it's like to come up as an outsider here, and I want more for them than that. What I've been thinking about, what I want to know is, can I invite them to join my House? There's got to be some kind of precedent for that when new Houses get established as part of a Turning, right?"

"Yes and no. I suspected this might be part of what you wanted to talk about, so I did some checking. Rules for new Houses are a bit different, but usually different in a way that supports the establishment of the House, including populating it with members."

"There's another but, isn't there?" Laurent asked.

"There is. Those new members are usually—almost exclusively—part of the Unseen World already. They tend to be members of already established Houses seeking to change allegiance, not outsiders. An entire House formed from outsiders would be unheard of. Is it explicitly forbidden? No. Would it be difficult? Almost certainly."

"What if they wanted to join another House? Dahlia Morgan has been teaching them, too, and they seem to like her."

"Dahlia Morgan? Really? I'm shocked."

Laurent laughed. "I was, too, but it's working out."

"Well, that's good." An edge of skepticism remained in her voice. "As to them joining House Morgan, they'd need to be formally invited by Dahlia, of course. But even then—House Morgan is established, and there aren't a lot of ways to join an established House outside of marriage or family."

"So, complicated. Again."

Grace nodded.

"Are those complications things that the current Head of the Unseen World is willing to change?"

"If I can, I will," Grace said. "Because you're right. They're magicians. There's no reason they shouldn't be allowed to join a House, if that's what they want. But it may not be possible by fiat—the Unseen World is interconnected in so many ways—in which case you'll have to play politics."

"This is where you tell me to get serious about an actual physical House, isn't it? I can do that."

"Good. You'll need one anyway, to have a place for the kids."

"You know, that's the first good reason I've heard to have one. No wonder you're the boss."

Grace gave an exaggerated roll of her eyes. "Since you're one of the very few who feels that way currently, I'll remind you to brace for pushback when you start this. The Unseen World doesn't like small changes on a good day, and what you're proposing is a great deal more than a small change."

"They haven't been happy about anything I've done." Laurent shrugged. "I'm not expecting this to be different."

"Doing it matters, though."

"It does. Enough to make sure this happens. Thanks, Grace."

It was time to put the pieces together.

The rebuilding of the House of Shadows had become

a thing of ongoing stasis. Pieces moved, realigned, shifted toward wholeness, but then moved away again, gathering in various combinations of almost but not quite. Magic had begun the process, had even accelerated it after Ian's death, but could not on its own complete it.

Dahlia had found magicians, sources of power, worthy sacrifices to magic, to the health of the Unseen World. She had taught them the necessary steps to offer that power, but it was diffuse, scattered, not gathering as it ought to, as it would, if there were a stronger focal point. There had been no change, not really, in the state of the Unseen World. Magic still had painful, inconvenient consequences for its use. The Houses were still falling apart, at the mercy of magic gone haywire.

The connection was the necessity. The House required magicians, and the magicians she found needed a House.

Dahlia was confident in her magic, but she hadn't wanted to interfere with whatever was happening on the island. Had wanted to give that strange rekindling spell the space it needed to take root on its own. So she had waited and watched until waiting no longer served a purpose.

It was time.

A chill wind followed Dahlia across the water to the island where the House of Shadows waited. She felt none of it. Neither the wind nor the dampness of the fog that clung to everything, seeping into joints and questing beneath surfaces for places it could cling to. She paid no heed to the cold, observatory moon.

The whole of her attention was on the island before her and what she would do there.

"That's it?"

Catriona's question snapped her from her reverie.

"Don't get me wrong—it's very horror movie and all of that, but I assume you plan to do more than just scare the magic out of them?"

Catriona was sleek and glossy, even in the middle of the night, like she was headed for a photo shoot, rather than to an abandoned island to perform strenuous magic. She was also, unfortunately, right about the current state of the island and what was on it. "That's why we're here."

Bones crunched beneath their feet as they stepped ashore and made their way to the center of the former House of Shadows. Catriona looked down at a particularly sharp snap, then curled her lip and side-eyed Dahlia. "Seriously, there is no reason that this can't be a normal sort of house with a yard that isn't made of dead people. I know aesthetics are not the priority, but this is ridiculous."

Once they arrived, Dahlia stopped. She took in the place. The slow, inexorable movement of the stones searching for wholeness. The stale, ancient scent of the air and the earth that blanketed so many dead. The electric hum of power vibrated around them. Potential. Waiting.

She waited, too, until she could feel it, all of what the House of Shadows had been and would be. Until every molecule of air around her was as known to her as her breath, until she felt in her own skeleton the frame on which her magic would be hung.

"Are you ready?" she asked.

She felt Catriona's focus snap into place. She was a strong magician, and Dahlia needed that power to support the work that was necessary here.

"Let's do this."

Dahlia held her spells, caught with thorns and complex as webs, in readiness. This was the proper place to cast them. Everything had to begin again here, at the beginning.

Breathing deep, she centered herself in the magic. She felt Catriona's power rise to meet hers, a support, a scaffolding.

She began the spell by calling the bones.

They were the true foundation of the House of Shadows: the remains of the magicians that had been given into its keeping. There was power in them still, power enough to build on, to anchor to. She sent her magic into the earth after them, questing, collecting. She pulled the dead from their rest and pressed them into service again.

The air grew heavy and thick, the pressure of a storm's leading edge, the burnt bitterness of ozone. The sky shaded to a flat, suffocating grey. Dahlia bound the bones in a lattice of power, strong as silver binding glass, making them no longer individuals but one incorporated thing. On this framework, everything else would rest.

Next, Dahlia turned her focus to the ruins. She called on their memories of wholeness and drew them together. Instead of mortar to seal the cracks between them, she used want. An emptiness that required an outside magic to fill it. Dahlia taught that emptiness the signs she had given to Laurent's students, taught it how to call magic away from the magician, to unwind it from them.

The broken stones of the House of Shadows recognized the want that flowed between them and bound them together. It was what they had always been: an empty, aching want. At the heart of the House, a need, a hollowness, a hunger. One that reached out to fill itself. One that would never be full, but would consume without ceasing as it tried to be.

Dahlia's spell set a seal on that wanting, made it sacred. The House of Shadows rejoiced in the blessing, strengthened itself with it.

Nauseated by the strain of all the magic flowing through her, she leaned harder on the support of Catriona's power. She dimly registered the other woman cursing at her, the pain in her voice, but her magic didn't falter, and the magic was what mattered.

She turned to the third and final part of the spell. The House raged when it realized what Dahlia intended, but she set her will against it, and her will was greater than all of its stone-held desire.

She gathered certain of the threads of magic that she had just made to channel power to the House of Shadows—one of three here, two of five there, odd numbered and off-balance—and cut off the House's access to them. She wove them together and then redirected them, connecting that magic elsewhere.

Connecting it to the Unseen World. Gathered from the sacrifice of magicians given for the strength of all. This was the magic that would restore that world to how it was meant to be.

The House of Shadows clawed back, pulling, panicked, against her, but Dahlia held the spell where she had shaped it, unpitying, unmoving. The pressure in the air shifted again, a deep and heavy sigh. A grudging acceptance.

Shaking, sweating, exhausted, and exhilarated, Dahlia opened her hands. Her spell was complete. Somewhere behind her, she heard Catriona collapse to her hands and knees, retching, but she had eyes only for what rose now before her. Not just scattered stones and partial walls, but a building, entire. Orderly. Organized. Complete.

The House of Shadows was reborn.

The crack of magic flung Sydney from sleep. She tumbled, sheets sliding from her grasp, and hit the floor. Scrambling, she made it as far as her hands and knees before the magic came again.

Stronger this time, immense, annihilating. Pressure behind her eyes, beneath her teeth, flooding her from the inside.

It licked like flames, tracing the patterns of her scars. The humid scent of a summer storm filled the air—petrichor, burnt ozone, and green, green, green.

An immensity, threatening to burst through her skin.

Sydney gritted her teeth, forced her breathing to a state that came close to imitating regularity. Her mouth tasted like wet, mown grass; green edged her vision. Acid etched its way through her bones.

Magic. It felt like magic. The pressure, the size of it.

She clambered to her feet, fumbling for the switch on her lamp, her shadow stretching across the moonlit wall.

Her shadow.

Sydney looked again, moving her hand as she did. The shadow made the same movement. She could see where it trailed from her fingers. Breath held, she shaped a spell with her hand, and with a snap, the lamp she had been reaching toward turned on.

Like magic.

Elation lanced through her. She was returned, whole. Once again herself. She had power, power that would let her stand against the House of Shadows and—this time—get it right. To make sure it would never come back again.

Then: "Oh fuck." The House of Shadows. The joy turned to ashes in her mouth.

She went to her kitchen, where she filled a bowl with water. She passed her hands over it, crossing and recrossing the cardinal directions. As she slanted her left hand east to west, an image bloomed on the surface of the water.

There it was. That had been the crack in everything that had woken her, the thing that had restored her magic. The House of Shadows.

Returned.

CHAPTER SIXTEEN

Sydney didn't go back to sleep. The idea of closing her eyes on what had happened was impossible, so she kept them open. She had tried to slide into an alternate comfort—to analyze, to plan—but that, too, proved impossible.

Shadows was back. Her magic had come back with it.

Dawn haloed the skyline, and Sydney winced as she gulped down coffee that had grown cold and bitter. She needed to see it. To put her hand in the miracle's side until she found the hidden rot. To test how tightly the gift was bound to the curse.

Mia wasn't exactly sure what she had come to Central Park to see. The thing she was most curious about—the House of Shadows—was hidden by a spell. She'd asked Ms. Morgan to teach it to her, but Ms. Morgan had said that the place needed to stay as secret as possible for now. The House, she had said, was healing, and it would heal more fully if left to do so undisturbed. Every reveal made it more likely to be noticed.

Which made sense. Mia barely needed magic to find the Agrippa Academy anymore. She just knew where it was, could feel its presence even before the spell revealed it to her sight.

Some of that was her own growing magic, but she knew now that some was also the imprint of the spell itself, a little more part of its surroundings every time it was used, leaving a little more of the sense that there was something there to look for, even if you weren't sure exactly what you'd find when you did.

She had seen people notice the spell, although they didn't know that was what they were doing, had seen them pause on that part of the sidewalk and look around as if they had lost something, or stare blankly at the place where there would have been a gate to the academy if they'd had the magic to see it.

It was weird, watching that happen. Part of her wanted to tell them—to lower the veil of the spell and show them what was hidden behind it. Part of her, the bigger part of her, wondered what she'd missed, before she'd learned how to see.

But even if she couldn't see the House of Shadows right now, maybe she could at least get a sense of it. Maybe she could start to know what its presence felt like in the world. Ms. Morgan had made it sound like something special—a place that was completely focused on and dedicated to magic. But it would be a lot, going there. She didn't know how long she would be able to stay, and she wouldn't be able to tell her family where she was. Mia wanted—she needed—something more direct, more real, before she made her final decision.

She shrugged into a hoodie and pulled the ends of the sleeves down over her hands. It had been warm earlier, but the temperature had dropped the farther she went into the park. The trees had gotten louder, too, rustling in the wind.

No. Not rustling. Not wind. Mia sketched a quick shape in front of her eyes, and mist rose from her hand like fog burning off in sunlight. A bitter, medicinal scent in the air and then a sense of sharpness, of clarity, as the world came closer into focus.

Not rustling at all. The trees were *talking*.

Speaking actual words, each tree in a different voice. Quiet, but like the wind she had first heard them as, carrying everywhere.

She saw the trees differently now as well. They seemed both more and less real. Unlike any trees she had ever seen, but also as if they could be no other way, have no close kinship to anything else.

Thin branched, and twisting like dancer's limbs. Flowers that looked like they had been carved, rather than grown, with off-white stone petals. Mia looked closer. No. Not stone. Bone. Petals made from bone, their fragrance that of a mausoleum's dust and secrets. And in the heart of each tree, more bones, set like the relics of the saints in her grandmother's church. Each different.

They were almost beautiful.

Mia walked through them slowly. She'd never seen magic growing wild like this.

It was clear that most of the other people in the park didn't see or hear the trees as she did. But as she watched, Mia could see their presence having an effect. People pulled their coats tighter around them, shoved their hands into pockets. They called out for the children they were watching play, gathered them in and hugged them close. Some brushed tears from their faces, as if they understood the words the trees spoke.

Mia did understand those words, and she understood, too, the people who wiped away tears and bent forward in postures of sadness as they walked by.

Mia wept as she listened. Ms. Morgan had explained to her how important it was to recognize the magicians who'd gone as sacrifices to the House of Shadows, who had given their magic to the Unseen World. She had called it a collective shame that they weren't better acknowledged and remembered. But hearing the voices now made it seem like more than a shame. It felt like a tragedy.

This was all those sacrifices had. They'd had to turn themselves into trees and grow in the middle of a public park, where most people couldn't see or hear them, to get anyone to notice them at all. Worse than that, Mia didn't see any other magicians here. No one stopping to listen, to remember, to honor. It was like an empty graveyard, not even flowers set against the stones. Her heart ached.

She stopped at the edge of the reservoir, looking out at what she couldn't see but knew was there. And still she heard the voices of the trees, a counterpoint to the water lapping at the shore.

Just sensing the House of Shadows wasn't enough. She needed to do more.

Mia stretched out her hands, reaching. Magic wasn't natural, not yet. She wanted it to be, but she still had to think about it, focus on it. The aftermath of each spell was still uncertain. Sometimes it was nothing more than a headache, or needing a nap. She got dizzy a lot. Once she threw up what felt like everything she had ever eaten and then had dry heaves for an hour. That had sucked.

And she kind of didn't care. Magic, power—it was worth it. Even if learning harder magic did mean that there were more consequences, like Ms. Morgan told her would happen, that was still worth it. For her, and for everyone who was now growing around her, leaves and bones and voices.

She sent her magic through her outstretched hands. She would find the House of Shadows through the veil of its spell, tell it she was here, that she was coming. Reassure it, and the voices in the trees, that they weren't forgotten.

The girl collapsed almost on top of Sydney's feet, the sharp bile scent of broken magic coming off her in waves. Sydney crouched, put her hand on the girl's shoulder. "Hey. Are you all right? Do you need anything?"

Mia blinked, trying to bring the face attached to the voice into focus. "No, I'm fine; I just . . ." Uncertain of how to complete the sentence without betraying what she had done, she let her voice trail off.

"Tried too much of a spell? Orange juice can help with the blowback, get your blood sugar up. There's a food cart nearby. I can go get you some, if you're okay to wait here."

Mia stared.

"You're one of Laurent's kids, right? Tried too much magic?"

And relaxed. "You know Mr. B? He's great. He mentioned the whole orange juice thing, yeah." Mia made it to sitting, paused before trying to stand. Whatever spell was hiding the House of Shadows was a lot stronger than the one around the academy, and it had *not* wanted to let her through.

"Take your time getting up," Sydney said. "Blowback can be a bitch. Can I ask what you were trying to do?"

"Just . . . to see something, I guess? To see it, and to tell it I was here."

Sydney's awareness sharpened. Impossible not to consider it, when she could feel Shadows leering behind her. She wasn't sure how much Laurent had told his students about the Unseen World's recent past, about the House of Shadows. But it had clearly been something, because this girl was here and was trying to find it.

And last night's developments had changed things. Shadows was no longer weak and partial. No longer on its own. Whoever brought it back would be trying to fill it. If it was strong enough, hungry enough, it might even be trying to fill itself.

"What were you looking for? Maybe I could help, show you a different way to cast the spell."

Something flashed across the girl's face, and her expression closed off. "No, it's fine. Thanks, though. Anyway, I'm feeling better. I should probably go."

Sydney handed the girl a folded-up bill. "Get the orange juice. My treat. I appreciate anyone who tries a spell so big it knocks them on their ass. You never know—it might've worked."

A cautious almost grin. "At least I didn't puke this time."

Sydney watched the girl go, making sure her feet were steady, and that she stopped at the food cart. Then she turned her attention back to the reservoir. Back to the House of Shadows.

She'd suffered through her own magical backlash earlier, attempting to cast a small spell against the House. It had reverberated back through her, confirming her suspicion: They were linked together. Her magic and Shadows.

It changed nothing: the House of Shadows and all it stood for could not be allowed to remain in existence.

It changed everything.

CHAPTER SEVENTEEN

When Sydney had made her previous plan to take down the House of Shadows, she'd had nothing but time. Every moment she'd spent in that place she'd spent plotting and dreaming of how to get out, how to fight back, how to win.

She had known Shadows, known Shara, almost as well as she knew herself. She had known what she was capable of, down to the slightest fraction of power. It hadn't been easy, what she had done, but it had been planned, precise. She had been the only person she'd had to account for.

This time, everything had changed, and kept changing, and she had an apartment full of people to worry about and far too many unknown factors, one of which was herself.

She hadn't wanted to tell the story more than once, and then had realized that she didn't want to tell it at all—it had been too long since she had felt like she could do something.

Sydney recast the scrying spell that she had done earlier that morning and revealed the House of Shadows. Casting it was easy—what a word that was!—magic, the gestures coming like muscle memory, pulling the power with them, leaving her space to observe, to watch the faces of her friends as they realized what she could do, as they realized what else had happened.

"But you can stop it, right? Or fight it, or whatever you did before. Sorry, I don't know the magical terms," Harper said. "You know how not to lose your magic now, so you can do this."

Sydney leaned against the wall. "The problem is it's not just a building I need to fight. Someone out there is helping that building, and there are people who show up in Grace's office and send her messages, wondering when she's going to make things normal again. Normal, in this case, meaning when Shadows was full of sacrifices being ground up for their magic.

"The problem is that even before whoever it was did the spell that tipped things from chaos to order, magic was trying to bring the House of Shadows back on its own. There is something in the Unseen World that wants that place to be there, and I'm not sure I do know how to fight that."

"There's another problem," Grace said.

"Of course there is," Sydney said.

"The Houses of the Unseen World are connected magically. I can feel them—I started being able to when I became the Head of the Unseen World. And now the House of Shadows is connected to all of them as well. I felt it snap into the spell and the spell become more stable when it did."

"Is this because I don't have a House yet?" Laurent asked. "It is, isn't it."

"There was a gap," Grace said, "and the House of Shadows filled it."

Laurent swore, low and vicious.

"Someone fit Shadows into that gap," Sydney said. "Let's not lose sight of that."

"So it really would be fighting against the entire Unseen World if Syd were to go after Shadows," Madison said.

"Very literally," Grace said. "I don't know what would happen to the other Houses. Or, quite frankly, to me."

Sydney felt a twist of relief combine with the knot of shame in her stomach. It wasn't just her, then. She wouldn't be the only one to face consequences if Shadows was gone. And maybe, if she figured out how to extract Grace from the spell that now connected her to Shadows, that would let her figure out how to extract herself from her own connection to the House. To extract herself, and still keep her magic.

"Madison, I want to go back to the archives," she said.

"That makes sense as a place to start. Harper, how do you feel about—"

Sydney cut her off. "No. No offense, Harper. But I want to go on my own."

"Even after last time?" Madison asked.

"Especially after last time. I think . . . I think the archives and I came to an understanding of sorts. I'd like to see if that understanding holds."

"I think she's right," Harper said. "I think she should go

alone. The archives paid attention to her in a way that was different than it reacts to me. Like listening to an equal, rather than humoring a kid sister."

"All right," Madison said. "Tomorrow. Early. You will bring me an enormous latte."

"Done," Sydney said.

"And you will also bring one for Harper, because I want her in the office, just in case."

"Early?" Harper asked.

"Done," Sydney repeated.

Sydney pulled Laurent aside as he was leaving. "There's one more thing you need to keep in mind. With Shadows being back, it's going to need sacrifices. And you happen to know a group of magicians who aren't affiliated anywhere. Which makes them fair game in the eyes of the Unseen World, since their mundane connections don't count."

"You think someone is going to come after my kids." His eyes sharpened.

"Or might be trying to already. I met one of them—amazing teal hair?"

"Mia."

"Mia. I met her at the reservoir yesterday. She had just tried some kind of enormous spell, which, probably thankfully, didn't quite work. She was trying to see something, she said."

"And if she was in that particular place, I have a good guess as to what she was trying to see."

"Exactly. Though, the thing I've been wondering is how she knew it was there to see. Are you teaching them history to go with their magic?"

"I have been, a little. Enough for them to know why the consequences of casting spells matter."

"So she could have figured out who the bone trees were, heard their voices, and decided to see what she could see. That makes sense."

"If anyone was going to go looking, it would be Mia, too." The corner of his mouth turned up, a quick smile.

"I liked her."

"She's pretty great. They all are. I'll send out a warning tonight, and work some kind of ward into the message to keep someone from being able to haul any of them off against their will. That place is not something to fuck with."

"No," Sydney said. "It's really not."

Dawn was just breaking through Madison's office windows as Sydney set a carrier with two lattes and a box full of pastries on her desk. "Apricot croissants and cardamom buns."

"Almost worth being awake this early for," Madison said. Harper's expression as she lunged for her coffee suggested that she disagreed.

"Do you want any of the stored spells, beyond what you need to manifest the archives?" Madison asked.

"No, I think just me and the archives today. Oh, and one

of those watches I enchanted to show the correct time." She turned to Harper. "Give me until noon before you check in."

"Not sure why you needed me here now, then," Harper muttered.

"Because while Sydney thinks everything will be fine, it is my job to plan for disaster, and your job, as my associate, to help me implement that plan, if needed." Madison smiled.

Harper blanched. "Right. Got it."

Sydney grabbed the spells needed to enter the archives. "See you on the other side."

The elevator ride went smoothly this time, and while using the stored spells was odd—seeing the effects of her magic without actually doing the casting made her feel as if there was still something she needed to do to finish the spell after she had triggered it, like a kind of magical jet lag—they worked as they should. The archives revealed itself and allowed her in.

She lit the candle that illuminated the archives, and the smell of fresh grass rose in the air as the wick caught, as the lights came up. The archives felt warm and welcoming. No sense of imminent tantrum, or any other sort of hostility. "Good morning," Sydney said, addressing the room generally.

As if in response to the greeting—and for all Sydney knew about the archives, that seemed fairly likely—a file drawer slid open in the far corner of the room. A clerk's light clicked on above it.

She nodded. "All right. Thank you. I'll start there."

The air in the room shifted to a state of studied disinterest, as if the archives didn't really want to concede that it was paying attention to what Sydney might find in that drawer. She was struck, again, with the feeling that there was a sentience behind the spell, like there was in the Houses. Those spells required a piece of the magician who cast them. It made sense that the same would have been true here, and that something of that magician might linger.

The first thing she noticed were the bones. Six, small and human. The remaining finger bones from the founding magicians, she guessed. She set them carefully on top of the cabinet, then took out the papers they had rested on.

The paper was old, the lines of time visible in the hand that had scribed it. Sydney read, then stopped halfway down the third page when the import of what she had found became inescapable. The realization hummed, electric, through her blood.

She looked up. "Thank you," she said, emphasizing the words. She read the pages once more, slowly, from the beginning. As she did, the feeling in the room altered. This time, to a sense of satisfaction.

Harper was waiting, stored spells in hand, as Sydney stepped off the elevator. "I was just about to come up and check on you. How did things go?"

Sydney smiled, wide and over-bright. "Harper! So great to see you. Is Madison in her office? Can you walk me over?" She nodded hello to an attorney leaning in the open door of a conference room, talking to a group sitting around the table inside. She recognized at least half of the people in the conference room from challenges during the Turning, and gossip was like air to the Unseen World.

Harper paused for a beat, then her expression shifted to match Sydney's bland pleasantness. "Of course. Just down the hall here."

Harper pulled Madison's door closed behind them. "Sydney, what—"

"Madison, is your office warded?" Sydney set the file, the bones on Madison's desk.

"Not fully, but I still have some of the wards you made."

"I'll cast one for now but start using those." Sydney thought for a moment, then spoke a word that sent a small wave of pressure through the office. The room's edges and corners blurred out of focus as the ward settled into place, then shifted to clear again.

Madison raised a brow. "What exactly did you find, Sydney?"

"The foundation spell for the Unseen World was tucked away in your archives. And by foundation spell, I don't just mean the instructions for casting. I mean there is literally a piece of that spell embedded in the papers in the file. This file." She opened it, showing the contents within.

The blood drained from Madison's face. "I need you to walk me through how you know this. In detail."

"Harper, get close enough that you can see, too." Sydney spread the pages out in rows, then tapped the one at the top-left corner. "Here. This page, with the signatures. There's a shimmer, a vibration in the ink. You can see it especially at the edges of the words. That's active, ongoing magic. And then there's the bones. Put them together, and you have an anchor."

"Wouldn't you need a dedicated building for that kind of spell, though?" Madison said, frowning as she looked over the pages. "Something solid enough to contain that sort of power."

"Here's the original deed to the land this building sits on." The same thirteen signatures written in ink with that same shifting, almost iridescent quality.

Madison looked up. "That does explain some things. The archives, for one."

Sydney nodded. "That hidden floor is the kind of thing that requires a tremendous amount of ongoing magical energy in order to maintain it. But if this spell is what the building sits on, then its existence makes a lot more sense."

"So this is a big, powerful spell," Harper said. "An old, big, powerful spell. But what exactly does it mean to have it? Like, if you light it on fire, does the Unseen World end?"

"I don't think it would be as simple as just lighting the papers themselves on fire—my guess is there are spells within spells—but yes, I think if they were destroyed, there would be significant consequences for the Unseen World.

"I'm just not sure yet exactly what those consequences would be."

"And I'm not sure why you feel like my desk is a good place for this, rather than leaving it where you found it." Madison's expression suggested she would have much preferred if Sydney had brought her something easier to deal with, like possibly a severed head.

"Because the archives made sure I found it. And then locked the drawer it had been in when I tried to put it back. So it may not belong on your desk, but it definitely doesn't belong up there anymore."

"You should keep it, Sydney. Take it home," Harper said. "If the archives gave it to you, then you need to have it."

"I agree," Madison said. "Take it home. Figure out what it means and why you need it there. Then let me know the next step in the plan."

"There's a plan?" Harper asked.

"There will be," Madison said.

"Yes," Sydney agreed. "There will."

Sydney had to brace herself against the shock when Verenice opened her door. The older woman looked worryingly thin and moved as if pain had settled into her bones.

Verenice couldn't hide her own astonishment. "Sydney! Your shadow! How?"

"I don't know, not exactly. But it's connected to Shadows, and that came back, too. There's a lot I need to tell you."

Verenice barely seemed to have heard her. She reached out, fingers pausing just before they would have passed through Sydney's shadow, then pulled back her hand. "I'm sorry. I was so surprised I forgot my manners. Please, come in, sit down."

Watching her progress through the house as she followed did nothing to reassure Sydney. Verenice seemed diminished somehow, hollowed out. "Are you . . . is everything okay?"

"Oh, of course it is. I've just been busy. And maybe a little under the weather, worrying so much about Shadows. It's fully back, then?" The older woman busied herself at the cupboards, setting out mugs, a pot. "Hot chocolate?"

"Thanks, yes. It is. Fully back, whole and entire. Missing only the sacrifices. Which, I think, will follow soon if we can't figure out who is helping it."

"How are you handling all of this?" Verenice handed her a mug.

"Everything I can do to stop it feels too slow. I'm starting too far behind. People are going to wind up in there again, Verenice.

"And then there's my magic. I should be thrilled. I *was* thrilled. I have never in my life been so happy as I was when I thought it had come back on its own, that I was healed. Then I realized that wasn't the case.

"What if that magic doesn't exist without Shadows? They came back *together*, Verenice. And I know, I know that

Shadows can't be allowed to continue. I have to figure out how to make sure it doesn't. I just—what if undoing it means I have to undo myself again? Now that I know what that's like, I don't know how I'll bear it." She drew in a ragged breath, then another. Set her mug down and walked across the room to the back door. She stood there, unseeing. Her shadow merged with others, blended. Impossible to separate one from the next.

Her voice when she continued was quiet, a confession. "I know this is cowardly, weak, but I want there to be another solution. I don't want it to have to be me again."

"I don't think that's weak, Sydney. I think it's honest. I want there to be another solution, too."

Sydney turned around. "Are you sure you're all right?"

"Goodness, I really must look terrible." Verenice smiled.

"It's not that," Sydney lied. "I'm just worried."

"I'm not something you need to worry about. But perhaps I will cut our visit short, and go have a nap."

"Of course. I'll be back in a few days, maybe the end of the week?"

Verenice considered. "Yes, that sounds perfect. I'll see you then."

Verenice had wrapped herself in a thick robe and gone to her garden after Sydney had left. She had felt almost undone herself when she had seen Sydney's shadow. Felt that all her work, all her sacrifice of magic and of self had been made redundant, unnecessary. Unuseful. Her heart had faltered with the blow, and still skipped and stuttered in its beats.

The moon silvered the leaves of the plants, turning them as beautiful as blooms against the night sky. It had rained that evening, and the clean, vital scent of damp earth lingered in the air. All around her were leaves unfurling, greening shoots, buds blossoming. Regrowth, return.

It was impossible to know what it would take to end Shadows this time, to know whether Sydney's magic would once again be the required payment. In the end, that didn't matter to the gift that Verenice wanted to offer her. A gift that meant that she wouldn't be the only one who was asked to sacrifice, a gift that meant that she wasn't alone.

That she wouldn't be alone, even when Verenice could no longer be with her. There was a relief in that, that something of herself would remain.

CHAPTER EIGHTEEN

Lara wondered if House Merlin was trying to drive her insane.

There was a whisper, somewhere. Everywhere. A woman's voice, she could tell that much. Sad, she thought. But beyond that, she couldn't hear it well enough to understand what it was saying.

She stood in different rooms, at different times of day, trying to decide if it was louder in the kitchen, or at three a.m., or when she was near a window. She listened so hard it hurt but couldn't tell any real difference, or at least not any difference she didn't change her mind about in the next room, on the next day.

She had asked House Merlin an entire list of questions about the voice and then, when she had gotten no useful answers, followed them up with an increasingly less polite set of requests to make it stop. Somehow. Please.

House Merlin insisted that it could not.

"What do you mean, you can't?"

The speaker isn't part of the House.

The House, she thought, had sounded smug. But since it had answered her while the whispering was happening, dispelling her theory that it was somehow the one talking, she supposed there was some truth to the response.

That didn't make her feel any better. In fact, the more she thought about it, the more it made her feel worse—a prank might have been preferable to a strange, unknown voice haunting her house.

She cast locator spells that refused to move from where she stood, amplifier spells that made every noise in the House louder except for the voice. She considered, briefly, some version of a spell that would render her unable to hear the voice but decided that the way her luck was going that would somehow become the only thing she was able to hear.

She nearly cried in relief when the House opened the door to let Grace in. "Thank you so much for coming. I feel like I am losing my mind."

Lara had reached out to Dahlia first, wondering if the voice was somehow a stray piece of magic left over from reconnecting House Merlin to the Unseen World, like a radio picking up an errant signal. But Dahlia had been busy, they kept missing each other, and so she asked Grace for help.

"Where is the most recent place you heard the voice?" Grace asked.

"It's in the hallway upstairs today—here, follow me—near

what used to be Miles' study. It seems to be there a lot." She opened her calendar app. "I started keeping track to see if I could find a pattern, and that's where it is about a third of the time."

The voice was still there, the melancholy tone a contrast to the warm, sunshine yellow she had painted the walls. Grace stood, focused, then shook her head. "I'd like to cast an amplification, if that's all right. So we can hear it better."

Somewhat trepidatiously, Lara agreed. "Sure, whatever you need to do." She addressed the House. "Please. We're trying to help."

Grace stirred the air with her hands, twice clockwise and once reversed. As she finished the third gesture, the air in the hallway grew cold and clear, and the voice resolved.

"It sounds like one of the bone trees," Lara said slowly. She had gone to listen to them, her passage through the park feeling like the least she could do to acknowledge the role her father and her family had played in their existence. But how would . . . "Oh no," she said.

Grace raised a brow.

"I think that's exactly what it is."

"It's possible that this is going to throw all the magic in House Merlin out of whack again, and I'd say I didn't care, but I do, except also, if that does happen, it might be for the best," Lara said as they walked down the stairs to the basement.

"Things have been difficult, with the House?" Grace asked.

"Difficult is an understatement. But I can't give up the hope that I can fix things."

"I kind of feel that way about the Unseen World as a whole."

A small, sharp laugh. "I can see that."

The voice was more intense by the cornerstone. Not louder or more understandable, but more present, more there. Lara felt the voice more than she heard it, even this close. A cold ache pressed just behind her breastbone, the sensation like the weight of held-back tears. "All right. I need to open this up."

She gathered herself to begin the spell, then stopped. Blew out a breath, let her hands fall back to her sides.

"Lara?" Grace asked. "Are you okay?"

She nodded. Then: "Hello, House. Look, I know things haven't been great. I'd like to fix that. Maybe this will help. I'm not sure it will, but I need to try. I'm sorry if it disturbs you. I'd do this another way if I could."

A pause, then a softening in the air.

More settled now, she called on her magic and opened the cornerstone.

The voice went silent.

A strange scent sighed out of the stone container—

staleness, salt tears, and something pale and fungal Lara couldn't identify.

The inside of the cornerstone no longer held neat, tidy rows of jars. Instead, it looked as if a small explosion had occurred.

Lara reached into broken glass, tarnished and snapped silver wire, and picked up a small, pale tree.

Roots coiled and curved, like hair, around her hand, seeking. It was not a particularly comfortable sensation. At the heart of the tree, a bone. Something impossibly small and delicate, only a shade darker than the roots.

In her hand, the tree spoke: *There was no light there, either. The thing I missed most was the sun.*

"She should be outside. In the sun. I should take her to Central Park with the others." Tears edged Lara's voice.

House Merlin spoke before Grace could say anything. *No. She should be here.* The tree relaxed in her hand: *Yes. I would like to stay.*

"Okay," Lara said. "Then you'll stay here."

The tree was small enough for the planting to be quick work. She looked happier already, Lara thought, with space to grow and the warmth of the sun to stretch toward.

"Thanks so much for helping me. For helping both of us," she told Grace when they were finished.

"If things keep going wrong after you reset your cornerstone, let me know, but I don't think they will. Not outside the current vagaries of magic, anyway."

"Oh, well, that should be totally fine, then," Lara deadpanned. Grace laughed and then left her alone with her House.

There was still the question of the cornerstone. She needed to replace the jars with something meaningful, a connection with the House.

"This would be a lot easier if you could just tell me what you wanted."

A quiet thump, and a book settled to the floor next to her. *Alice's Adventures in Wonderland.* The copy Ian had given her. The one she had asked the House, again and again as she tested its magic, to bring her.

She set her hand on the book's cover, the texture as familiar as fingerprints. Something that mattered to her, that reminded her of Ian, of his kindness. A story that felt like home. "For the cornerstone?" she asked House Merlin.

The book rose beneath her hand, then slid forward, settling in.

"Not the thing I would have guessed or chosen," Lara said. It was an ache, to think about that book locked away. Not because there was no other way to read the story—she could download a new edition on her phone in less time than it would take to cast the spell to reseal the cornerstone. It was the tangible connection to what that particular copy of the book meant to her, the memories it held. The love it was given with. Ian.

It was an ache that meant the House was correct in its choice. That this was exactly what she wanted the foundation of House Merlin to rest on.

Lara sniffed, wiped tears from her eyes, from where they had fallen on the cover of the book.

"All right. Let's try this again."

CHAPTER NINETEEN

The building loomed up, out of mists and nowhere, appearing with the suddenness of a sprung trap. Mia shivered, rocking the boat beneath her feet. It was colder here than it had been on the shore, as if the island generated its own weather. She glanced at Ms. Morgan, but the older woman looked as calm and poised as ever, as if she was impervious to minor things like the temperature.

Mia wished that she could be that calm, but she was seasick with nerves, like a mass of eels had taken up residence in her middle. Still, she squared her shoulders and schooled her expression. She didn't want to give even the slightest hint that she wasn't ready to be there. Now that she had made her choice, she wouldn't give any reason for it to be taken from her.

She had made her preparations along with her choice, had cast spells over family and friends so that when they thought of her, they would think they had just seen or heard from her, would seem to remember that they had texts and messages she had just sent. She didn't want anyone to look for her, and she didn't want anyone to worry. Ms. Morgan had told her that was a clever piece of magic, and that had felt like further proof that Mia was making the right choice.

Her smooth expression slipped when she stepped onto the island itself. The ground shifted beneath her feet, dirt heaving up and falling away to reveal a skull. Mia gasped and yanked her foot back from where she had been about to step.

"The island is still adjusting." Ms. Morgan continued walking, as if this was only to be expected. "It's been through a lot of changes recently."

Changes. Changes that involved skulls popping up out of the ground. That was fine. She could do this.

When she had told Ms. Morgan that she wanted to go to the House of Shadows, Ms. Morgan explained that magic was different there, not what she had been used to so far. That it would be more present, more intense. She hadn't mentioned all the skeletons, but Mia could handle things being a little more dramatic than she had prepared for.

The ground crunched beneath their feet, and she resolutely did not consider what, precisely, was making the sound.

"Here we are," Ms. Morgan said.

Mia couldn't quite fix her gaze on the building itself. She blinked, rubbed her eyes, searching for focus, but it was as if the structure in front of them was fogged, blurred. The edges between it and the air were fuzzy, amorphous.

Then she realized—not fog. Shadows. Great gatherings of them, even in places where the angles of the light should have made it impossible. They draped the building like shrouds. Hiding. Concealing.

And then the building moved. Physically, literally moved.

Shadows gathered at the front of it, a deeper black, like that of an unlit subway tunnel. Inside that blackness, something opened.

Mia's hard-won cool fled, and a half shriek escaped her mouth. "Oh my God."

A smile flickered across Ms. Morgan's face. "Welcome," she said, "to the House of Shadows."

It was colder still as Mia stepped inside, and while the door had appeared silently, it shut itself behind them with a horror movie grind of stone against stone. It was the sound of a choice that couldn't be undone, a signpost of no way out. This was what she wanted, she reminded herself. She had chosen to be here, to stay as long as she was needed.

Ms. Morgan said a short phrase under her breath and flung her left hand up. Her spell scorched the air, leaving a bitterness at the back of Mia's throat. Balls of light flared into being. Although the globes were bright, their light didn't quite reach all of the building. Shadows still gathered and clung, seemingly at random. More than there should have been, in impossible places.

There was nothing in the room besides the light and shadows. No furniture, no blankets, no food. No nothing that suggested that people were meant to stay there any length of time, or that suggested that even their brief presence was welcome.

"Why does it have to be here?" Mia asked, her words an echo in the emptiness.

Ms. Morgan turned an assessing look on her, as if wondering whether bringing Mia here had been a mistake after all.

"Why any particular place, really?" Mia continued. "You said there are spells to channel the magic that belongs to the Unseen World. So what's different about my doing those spells here, instead of in my room at home or in your class?"

"This is a place that focuses magic, concentrates it. Some of the spells you'll do here aren't any different from the ones you could do in your bedroom, it's true. But here, the benefit of casting them will be far greater. In the same way, the magic you learn here—and you will learn magic here, magic only the House can teach you—will be stronger."

She paused. "You don't have to stay here, Mia. I know I'm asking a lot. If you want to leave, tell me now. I promise I won't think any less of you."

Mia considered. The shadows did, too, looming close as they waited for her choice. "You said the magic that I learn here will be stronger. Is that true just when I'm casting spells here, or will I still be more powerful even after I leave?"

"No, the strength will always be there. Any magic that you take away from here will always be yours."

"Then I'm staying," Mia said.

The listening shadows receded and coiled in their corners, content.

Nothing went how Mia expected. Ms. Morgan had told her not to bring anything with her—no food, no changes of clothes, no items of comfort from home. "The House will provide."

She repeated that now, emphasizing that this was part of how Mia would bond with the House. If she couldn't convince the House to give things to her, then she wouldn't have them.

The thought crossed Mia's mind that no food or water or toilets was really more than she had signed up for. She might have almost changed her mind and asked to leave then, had Ms. Morgan not been looking at her with an expression that suggested that was exactly what she expected Mia to do. Instead: "I can do this," she said, fronting a confidence she didn't feel. "I want to."

Ms. Morgan had nodded and said she'd be back to check

on her progress. That was a relief at least. No way Ms. Morgan had brought her here just to starve to death. It made sense that if things didn't work right away, she'd help Mia until they could. And while she hadn't specifically said that Mia could leave whenever she wanted, she definitely could, if she was willing to fail. It's not as if she was going to be locked in.

Then she left, and Mia was alone.

She had known she would be, that Ms. Morgan couldn't stay in the House of Shadows with her.

"This House is like all of the other great Houses. It needs someone to bond to, someone to hold its magic," Ms. Morgan had explained. "Perhaps, if the House accepts you, you could be that person. It's an important responsibility."

Mia wanted to be that person. To hold the House, it was called. It would mean that she was important—a powerful magician, necessary to the Unseen World. That was part of why she'd agreed to come here, to leave her own home to stay in the House of Shadows. It was so the House could get to know her, could decide if she was worthy.

There were a lot of parts to why she'd agreed to come here, agreed to stay, but that was the most important right now. She had to convince the House to accept her.

"Just start by introducing yourself," Ms. Morgan had told her. "You'll know if the House is listening."

Mia stood in what seemed to be the center of the House.

It was an enormous space, high ceilinged and open. Grey, stark stone everywhere. No hint of comfort, or of softness. Even the lights that Ms. Morgan had cast were fading.

This was a place that wouldn't give so much as a fraction, but would force any inhabitants to carve out whatever scraps they could. There was no hint of weakness, either. Maybe that was what mattered, that proof of strength.

"Hello," Mia said.

Sometimes, in open spaces, a voice seems to travel. To seek out corners and quiet places to fill. Not here. Mia spoke her introduction, and her voice stopped, as if her words fell out of her mouth to crumble at her feet.

That reaction did not feel particularly welcoming.

"My name is Mia."

That same flatness in the air after she spoke. Not like the House wasn't listening, but like it was deliberately ignoring her.

Mia shivered, pulling her sleeves over her hands, then wrapping her arms around herself. Her breath came in puffs of frost, and she wished she had worn something warmer than her hoodie.

She turned in a circle slowly, taking in the entire space. There was no sign that the House was in any way interested in her. This was not encouraging. But there was no way she was letting Ms. Morgan down. There was no way she was letting herself down.

Though it would have been nice if she had been given some sort of instructions, a how-to guide. It wasn't like Mia had a lot of experience introducing herself to magic houses.

Magic houses.

She was here because she was a magician. Here to learn magic, and to do it. The House of Shadows wasn't going to care what her name was if she didn't also show it what she could do.

Mia thought back on what she had learned, and then she formed the shape with her left hand that would channel part of her magic here, to the House, and out to the Unseen World. The part of the magic that she offered as sacrifice.

As she readied the rest of her spell, she felt the air around her change, one small corner of the House's ostentatious ignoring of her becoming a sort of covert attention. That was good. Maybe this might actually work.

She spoke a word that crackled at the back of her throat and tasted like licking matches, and then traced her name in the air. When she finished, fuchsia letters, bright and whirling as sparklers, appeared.

A pause.

The air changed again, that covert attention becoming a fully focused awareness, as if enormous spotlights had clicked on to illuminate her.

In a different hand, in letters made of dripping shadows: *Hello*.

"One?" Catriona asked. "You put one magician into the House of Shadows. One. We did all that work, we need so much power right now, and you put one barely trained outsider high school kid in there thinking that would fix things."

She was a bright flame of color against the quiet neutrals of Dahlia's living room. Leaning forward from the edge of the couch, frustrated intensity directed at Dahlia like a child with a magnifying glass hovering over ants.

"The House needs someone to be there, to be in charge of it," Dahlia said.

"Sure, fine, I get that. But one? One person, Dahlia. Why not just take Laurent's little class of misfits on a field trip and leave them there? Put her in charge if it makes you feel better, but she's not enough by herself. The Unseen World needs power and it needs it now, or have you forgotten that our Houses are literally falling down around us?"

"I'm aware, thank you." The falling leaves in House Morgan's entryway were constant now, and that was the least annoying thing that was happening in her House. "But part of the reason that the Unseen World was weakened was that Miles took shortcuts. I want to make sure to do things properly."

"The problem with Miles wasn't that he took shortcuts, it

was that he fucking stole from us and lied about it. Very different." Her words sharp, impatient.

"If he hadn't taken the shortcuts, he wouldn't have been able to steal from us, because we would have noticed something going wrong. Getting things right this time matters."

"No, getting things done now matters. You need to move fast, or you won't have a chance to get things right. Everything needs to be in place before Laurent figures out one of his precious kids is missing and asks where she went. Before someone heads out to the island to check on what's up out there, and Mia steps out of Shadows to say hi. You need to make sure no one can stop this. Then you can sit back and worry about the details."

Dahlia pinched the bridge of her nose, a probably futile attempt to cut off the headache she could feel gathering.

"You know I'm right."

Dahlia wasn't quite ready to concede that completely, but Catriona's points weren't ones she could afford to dismiss, either. "Then offer me someone from House Don to take to Shadows."

"Nope. No chance. And for the same reason you aren't rushing over there with some barely magical Morgan third cousin. You won't, I won't, the rest of the Unseen World won't until we're sure this works. Works, and is locked in this time, so that none of Sydney's little gang of do-gooders can fuck things up."

Dahlia didn't like it. It felt messy, like cutting corners. But people would start to notice things like students missing from classes and the consequences of magic easing, and as they noticed, they would talk. Things could get complicated if the wrong people noticed too much. It would be easier to show them that she was right and that things would be better if they listened to her if things *were* better, and she needed a fully functioning House of Shadows for that. The headache pressed harder.

"Fine," she said. "You're right. I'll bring in the rest of the kids."

CHAPTER TWENTY

There were no consequences to this magic.

Sydney raised her hands, and the pages of the file she had taken from the archives rose as well, hanging in the air. She made adjustments—sharp, quick gestures, the swipes and pinches of manipulating data on a touch screen that here moved papers that were hundreds of years old around her apartment. As easy as thought.

No matter what kind of spell Sydney did, no matter how much magic it required, there were no aftereffects. Magic was as easy, as uncomplicated as breathing. It was intoxicating.

It was terrifying.

This was how magic had been for the Unseen World before she had cut them off from the House of Shadows. No wonder they hated her.

She couldn't think about it; she thought about it all the time.

It made no sense. If anything, there should have been increased consequences or some other sense of payment for her magic, if its return was connected to Shadows. Shadows wasn't inhabited. It had no magic to feed on. It should have been ravenous.

There had been no change in anyone else's ability to cast spells without payment, no shoring up of the foundations of the crumbling Houses. Magic hadn't changed. Only she had. But she couldn't see a way to sever the change in her from the return of Shadows.

The problem of magic, of Shadows, of connection was all-encompassing. Not only for her role in it but for the way it wove through the entire Unseen World. The founding spells had wanted that connection, had prioritized that interweaving. She was only a symbol of that desired outcome.

That had been Verenice's thought. That perhaps Sydney was given her magic as a counterweight to Shadows, that she was meant to act as a balance. If magic had brought one back, why not the other? But that didn't answer the question of why magic had allowed Shadows to return at all, thus making that counterweight necessary.

Sydney felt reduced to a game piece in an unseen hand.

She hated that. Hated feeling as if she still wasn't her own, as if her life was being determined by some old signatures and a pile of bones. She turned back to the papers set out across her table, back to the spell that bound them all together, back to her plan to unweave.

Sydney tilted back in her chair and pressed her hands to her eyes. "It feels like my brain is a knot. That knot, specifically." She gestured to her wall, where an enormous multicolored tangle of yarn hung.

"Which is why I brought over my own weight in Chinese food," Madison said. She had already unpacked three containers, and there was a second full bag on the counter.

"Did you get—"

"Extra shrimp noodles? Yes. And you're going to take a break and eat them before you tell me why you've tied an entire sheep's worth of yarn to your wall."

"It's the spell. I'm trying to—"

Madison handed Sydney a plate of food. "Eat. First."

"Can we eat and talk?" She winced at Madison's expression. "It's just that talking it through will help my brain relax."

Madison sighed. "Fine. But you will eat. It's like negotiating with a toddler, I swear."

Sydney nodded her thanks as she swallowed a dumpling. "It's why the yarn wall. I need to see the spell in order to figure out how to take it apart, and this is the easiest way to see it."

"The easiest. Okay, but right now, it just looks like an enormous knot, Syd."

"That is one of the problems, yes."

"And I'm guessing that if just cutting through it were an option, you would have done that already."

"It's completely interwoven. Hang on. I'll show you." Sydney scooped up a mouthful of spicy peanut noodles, then shoved containers of food out of the way and laid out sheets of paper in their wake.

"Sydney, are those the original documents?" Madison's voice idly curious.

"What? Oh, yes. What else would they be? Just a second." She rearranged two of the pages.

"There are soup dumplings resting on the foundation spell for the Unseen World."

"I'm sure it's known worse. Anyway, the spell starts here, in the paper itself. There's magic literally woven into the fibers. And then knotted with that is the visible text of the spell. It's so clever, the way it's set down. There are interconnected threads from the letters, from punctuation, even from things like this, that look like they're just blotches of ink or strike-throughs of mistakes."

"And how much of your yarn wall is that, roughly speaking?"

"The blue. I color-coded the layers of the spell."

Madison narrowed her eyes and considered the wall. "There's not a lot of blue there."

"Like I said, it's really interwoven. Maybe the strongest, most elegantly constructed piece of magic that I've ever seen." It was astounding, really, the planning that had gone into making it. Had circumstances been different, she would have loved to talk to the magician who had designed it. She was sure it had only been one, though casting would have taken more than that. There was something unifying, similar, about the choices made in the magic.

"Great." Madison shook her head. "Okay, what's next?"

"The bones. Well, the first set of bones."

"Because of course there's more than one set."

A grin flashed across Sydney's face. "Of course. The direct connection from the pieces of the spell in the papers is to the finger bones we found in the archives, which then connect to the skeletons in the foundations of the Houses. That one's enhanced with natural sympathy, because the bones in the archives belong to those skeletons. But then, the connection to each House is also another independent part of the spell. These are the red threads, and then the black. The grey is where the spell anchors back into your offices, and then the archives themselves."

"And the yellow, that's sort of on top of everything? What is that for?"

"Memory. This is an old, powerful spell. It's used to existing. It would rather continue to do so."

"So what happens if you pull a thread? Magically speaking, I mean."

"Pretty much the same as if you pulled one of the threads on my wall. Actually, you know what? Go ahead."

Madison looked at the mass of yarn pinned to the wall, then pulled a dangling black thread. A squeeze, a shudder. Space between the lines of thread disappeared. "It all got tighter."

Sydney nodded.

"But you said black was for the Houses. There's one missing—Laurent hasn't founded his yet. So that should be the weakest part of the spell." It was why she had chosen that particular thread—it looked like it was least likely to have an effect on anything else.

"Except that there are thirteen Houses if you count Shadows. Remember, Grace felt the Houses readjust when Shadows came back fully."

Madison looked troubled. "But Shadows wasn't one of the original thirteen. And it doesn't participate in the Turning. So it shouldn't be bound into this part of the spell, if I'm following you correctly."

"You're right. But there is a gap in the spell, because Laurent hasn't founded his House yet. And magic saw a way to fill it. So it did."

"I didn't know magic could do that."

"It doesn't, usually."

"That is . . . that is a strong spell, Sydney."

"There's one other thread. One that I haven't woven in, because I'm not sure yet exactly how it connects." She took a deep breath. "Mine."

"You're still certain that your magic is connected to Shadows now." Madison set down her chopsticks.

"I think that I have to assume that it is, and that ending one will mean ending the other."

Madison met Sydney's eyes, held them. "Are you going to be able to do that?"

"I've been asking myself that question. Because I know what needs to be done. I know Shadows is evil; I know that the world where it is allowed to exist is wrong. I know that I can't live with myself if I don't do whatever I can to end both of those things."

"But?"

"But I wish this wasn't a decision I had to make. I wish it could be someone else—and yes, I get that wishing someone else could do the hard part is how we got Shadows in the first place."

"That's not quite the same, Syd."

"Isn't it? I'm hoping that as I figure out how to undo this spell"—she waved her chopsticks at the snarl of yarn on the wall—"I'll figure out how to unwind myself and my magic from it. I have to believe that's possible."

"And if it isn't?"

Sydney looked at the mass of interconnected threads. "I know what I have to do."

CHAPTER TWENTY-ONE

Laurent had kept almost all of them safe.

The wards he had placed on his students had triggered, exactly like they were supposed to, when that treacherous bitch Dahlia Morgan had tried to feed them to the House of Shadows. They had kept them out of her clutches, alerted him to the attempt.

He had not planned for one of them to have chosen to go to Shadows of her own free will. He hadn't thought to protect against that.

He ran, now, through Central Park.

He'd texted Sydney as soon as he'd learned where Mia had gone but didn't want to wait for her, didn't want Mia locked away in that place any longer than she had to be.

He wasn't sure he'd ever hated anyone the way he hated Dahlia Morgan at that moment. "It was her choice," she'd said, when he'd confronted her. "I gave her every opportunity to change her mind."

Laurent skidded to a stop in front of the reservoir, looked around for a boat, a bridge, whatever it was that brought people over to the island, then realized that of course there was no need for a permanent structure when the only people who were meant to go there were magicians. "Get it together, Beauchamps," he muttered to himself. He needed to. This was the place that had killed Ian, had done so even before being restored to full strength. If he was going to get Mia out of there safely, he needed to focus.

He cast a spell that hardened the water beneath his feet and began to run again.

Ten feet from the shore, something beneath him yanked his footing away, dropping him into the water.

After that, things got bad.

Laurent was dragging himself out of the reservoir when Sydney arrived. He paused, bent over, hands on his thighs, and vomited a stream of brackish, foul-smelling water. There were small cuts covering his hands and forearms, and a larger one, crusting over, that slashed through his left eyebrow.

She ran to him, helped him steady himself. "What happened?"

"Shadows. I can't get to it. It won't let me. There's some sort of spell protecting access to the island, and it's one I'm not good enough to get through. It came close to drowning me. I barely got back here."

"The rest of your kids are safe?"

"The wards worked, so I think so. For now, anyway."

"All right. I'll go see if I can get Mia back. I don't think

Dahlia would try the same thing again—she knows you'll have extra protections on the kids now. So let's force her hand. Go to Grace, in her capacity as Head of the Unseen World. See if there's anything official she can do to stop Dahlia, now that we know who is helping Shadows. You two are good at that side of things." Laurent was like she was, she knew. He'd feel better if he was doing something.

"Got it. Done. Syd, be careful. That place is vicious."

She nodded. "It always was."

Sydney watched Laurent hurry away before turning her attention back to where the House of Shadows waited.

The House of Shadows with Mia Rodriguez inside it.

It felt simultaneously impossible and inevitable, to be back here like this. She didn't know Dahlia Morgan, didn't think she had ever encountered her during the Turning. But the who wasn't really the issue—never was. Of course someone would think that Shadows had been needed, had been right and good. After all, someone had made it in the first place. Generations of someones had gone along with it. Had sent children there as sacrifices, had used the magic that resulted. If it hadn't been Dahlia, it would have been someone else.

Her hand went to the small box of matches in her pocket. She had grabbed them on her way here—the spell that had ferried her back and forth from Shadows before had begun with a lit match. She'd hated everything about that spell.

It would work again. Sydney knew that in her bones.

If Shadows was hiding itself, maybe it would be easier to get there if she arrived on its terms. But then, if Shadows didn't want her there, it would try to keep her away no matter what she chose.

So instead of calling the boat that had always seemed like it was ferrying her to hell, the boat that she knew Shadows would make sure arrived still stained with Ian's blood, she used her own magic to make her way there.

She reached for what had fallen, the detritus that had slid beneath the surface, sunken and resting. She called it up—waterlogged tree branches and lake plants and various things hidden in the water as secrets. She wove them together, and she made a bridge.

Her path across was swift and sure. None of the difficulties she had been braced for Shadows to inflict on her occurred. There was only the bridge and the water and then the shore of an island built on bones.

She felt them as she stepped onto the island, the dead, the remnants of their magic sunken in the earth. The hoard of a cursed dragon. In front of her, crouched at the center, the revenant monster that sat atop them: the risen House of Shadows.

At its core, hunger. A gaping maw in place of a heart. It would swallow all the world's magic, if it could, and then gnash its teeth searching for more. That kind of hunger was never satiated. It only increased.

The facade shifted and changed as she watched, moving through shape after shape as if trying on hats. And then it stopped. Held. It let the cracks in the building show, lines of fracture from where she had brought Shadows down before. Maybe it thought to show off. To demonstrate that it was whole again. To show that it remembered what she had done, and that it no longer cared. After all, it had risen and been made new.

But if the magic remembered what it was to be whole, that meant it also remembered what it was to be broken. More important, Sydney remembered breaking it. Separating stone from stone and unmaking what never should have been. She knew the feeling in her very bones. She knew what she had done before. She knew what she would do again. She would remind Shadows of what it was to break.

And unlike the magic that had rebuilt the House of Shadows—all along the same lines, a carbon copy of what had been before—Sydney had learned from her mistakes.

Shadows had settled into place with its doors open. It never did care about keeping people out.

Sydney steeled her spine and walked back in.

Mia wasn't sure how long she had been in the House of Shadows. There was nothing like a schedule here. Impossible to measure the passage of time, or even tell night from day, and all she knew about sleep and food was that she was seriously behind on both. She had no phone, no internet. It was just her and the House and the magic.

The House loved showing her magic.

Mia curled her hands into fists, then flexed her fingers, stretching them open as far as possible. They were numb most places, and full of pins and needles where they weren't, like they were unthawing. It felt weird, but also kind of great. Like she could literally feel her ability to do magic growing. She had never cast spells like this before. The kind of magic she had come here to learn.

The kind of magic that could have saved her sister.

She knew, now, with the aftershocks of her spells still firing along her nerves, that she could do the sort of magic that would stop a bullet, save a life. And that it was worth—

she fell to the floor, muscles seizing with spasms as if an electrical current ran through her. The air went hot and blue white, and her own breath scorched her lungs. Her teeth ground together so hard that screaming was impossible. A minute? Two? When it ended, she felt as if she had been pulled inside out

—all the consequences. Breathing hard, trembling, she picked herself back up. That sort of magic was worth staying there to learn, no matter how hard actually living there was.

She asked the House for food. The spells she had done had left her shaky, light-headed, as if she hadn't eaten in days. Shadows responded with something that might have once thought about being bread and cheese but certainly bore no resemblance to either now. Still, she felt less frantic as she choked it down, and so Mia ate.

She hadn't quite figured out the right way to ask the House for food yet. It never seemed to understand what she wanted, and what it gave her was often burnt, or half-raw, or cold where it should be warm. But she'd get better. Things would be easier then. She'd figure out how to have a comfortable life here, once she understood the House more. She just needed to work harder. She could do that.

Her stomach was a hollow, uneasy churn. Her joints ached like the inside of bruises. Mia leaned her head against a wall and let her eyes flutter closed.

Up! Now!

The House. Excited, insistent.

She's coming—she's here!

Something else in the House's voice, too, Mia realized as she scrambled to her feet. She wasn't quite sure what.

And then she had no more time to think about it. The door to the House opened. In it, the figure of a woman, a shadow against the sky.

The shadow walked in.

CHAPTER TWENTY-TWO

The inside of Shadows was not what it had been when Sydney had been held within its walls. It had been a changeable place then, capricious and cruel, but orderly. Shara's will had been iron, and the House had not gone against her. It had been a prison, yes, but it had also been recognizably a house, with shape and structure. Walls and rooms, doorways and locks. The spontaneous changes it had made had been within Shara's bonds, done to serve her purpose.

What Sydney saw now was chaos. A shell of a place, no more than that. There were no rooms here, no structure. The only walls were those that formed the barrier between inside and out. It was a strange sort of realization, that all the effort Shadows had put into rebuilding itself had come only to this.

The detritus of magic was scattered everywhere. The air had the charred-iron scent of spells that had consumed more than they were meant to. Smudged letters in the dark brown of dried blood streaked the walls, and the tips of Sydney's fingers ached in sympathy. She knew the desperation that drove that kind of writing.

"Ms. Morgan said you would come." The voice cracked

and rasped, as if it had been speaking words too raw for its throat to endure. The voice too full of bravado, and almost unbearably young.

"Then I'm assuming she also said that I'd tell you that you should leave, because in all likelihood, Shadows will kill you if you stay. That's who all the bones are, the ones in the ground that you walked over when you came here. All the people Shadows killed the last time it existed. I'm only the second person who lived, who was able to force the doors open and leave." Sydney scanned the room as she spoke, looking for Mia. There was a shape in the shadows, tense and anticipatory. Sydney shifted her gaze there but walked no closer.

"She told me you wouldn't understand why I was here."

"She was right. I don't. I don't understand why anyone would voluntarily put themselves here. Not if they knew what this place was. What did she tell you to make you think this was a good idea?"

"Don't patronize me." A gesture, rough, that swirled and thickened the shadows where they stood, and then the scent of scorched hair bloomed, thick and choking as the spell died unborn.

Mia's shock was enough to drop her veil. She looked dramatically changed from the girl Sydney had met only days ago, tangled and haunted, her eyes fever-bright, astounded that her magic had failed to obey her.

"You're right," Sydney said. "The spell should have worked.

Especially here, with Shadows and all its magic to help you. You did it right. There's just more to magic than that."

Sydney had felt the rebound and recoil of Mia's spell as if on a time lapse, the shake and stutter of the magic as the spell fizzled out. Had felt the House swallow her spell, the hunger of it, overlaid with glee at sabotaging the girl.

There was still separation between the two, then. Shadows hadn't fully decided to align itself with Mia. That might make it easier to get her out.

"And there's more to me than you think. I'm here because I want to be. Because I *chose* this." Determination in every line of her body, even as she swayed on her feet from exhaustion.

"I'm sure it was your choice. I just don't think you would have made it if you had been given all the information."

"You really don't get it, do you?" Mia let the rest of the shadows fall away from her. She was hollowed, thinned, twisted wire-tight. "I'm not ignorant and I'm not stupid. I knew this wouldn't be an easy thing. But I also know what I want from magic, and I know what I'm prepared to sacrifice for it.

"You haven't even bothered to ask me why I'm here. You just assume you know better and tell me to leave."

Sydney pushed her sleeves back, showing her scars, the places where magic had been cut out of her, again and again, during her years in Shadows. "Did Dahlia tell you how the sacrifices were made? How magic was carved out of us? That the reason the dead were dumped into the dirt was so that the

House could continue to extract what little magic remained in their bones? Did she tell you that we were brought here as babies, as children? That not one of us ever had a choice?"

"All of that happened because the magic that this House made was corrupted. People used it for the wrong reasons. I'm helping it return it to its true purpose." Mia shone with the vehement certainty of true belief.

"Magic *was* corrupted," Sydney said. "You're right. But the solution to that isn't bringing back Shadows. The creation of the House of Shadows was the heart of that corruption in the first place."

"I can understand how you would think that." Mia's voice a rasp that grated the air. "Your sacrifice wasn't acknowledged, and that was wrong. But mine will be, and I'll make sure they all are, from now on."

Sydney changed tack. "Mia, people are worried about you."

Anger sharpened her words like teeth. "Now I know you're lying. I set up spells so no one would even know I was gone."

"Laurent found out. He's blaming himself—he feels like he failed you. He almost drowned trying to get here."

A flinch, then, briefly: "I'm sorry for that, but he should understand why this matters."

"All right. Then that's what I'll tell him. That this was your choice, and your mind is made up to stay."

"It is."

Sydney nodded and turned for the door. Then snapped back around, flinging a spell at Mia as she did.

The stutter-step-echo feeling of too-proximate magic hit her first. Knocking her sideways, disorienting her. Her spell slammed into an invisible wall in front of Mia, crackling and shattering into uselessness. It crashed to the floor in shards, leaving the air reeking of rotting compost.

She had a second to register the shock on Mia's face. Not her magic, then. Shadows'.

A sensation like a hand reaching into her center and pulling. Sydney flew.

Then fell.

Landed.

Face pressed to earth. To bone.

Slowly, aching, Sydney pulled herself to her knees. The wall of Shadows rose before her.

It no longer had a door.

A sharp, surprised laugh broke from Mia's mouth when Sydney disappeared. It was as if the House itself had decided it had had enough. Mia waited, watching, skin goose-bumped from adrenaline, for the door to reopen, for Sydney to reappear, but there was nothing.

She was just . . . gone.

Sydney was gone, which meant that she had won and the House had protected her, worked with her to do what she wanted, just like Ms. Morgan had said it might. This was why she had come here. This was exactly what was supposed to be happening.

This was amazing.

Mia ran to the wall, looking for a window, wanting to see Sydney's reaction.

There was no window. Mia stepped back, looked again. No window, and also, no door.

"Hey, can you let me see out there at least?"

Nothing happened.

Mia sighed.

The House seemed to rearrange itself whenever it got bored. She'd have to figure out where it had hidden the door this time.

She put her hand to the wall and walked, without lifting it, until she returned to where she started. She looked up, scanning the heights of the walls, the ceiling, then casting spells to illuminate, spells to reveal, and then casting them again, even as the use of magic drained so much of her energy that it left her nauseous and trembling. She walked over every inch of the floor, then lowered herself to her hands and knees to check again at a crawl.

"Okay, ha ha, very funny, now where's the door?"

Only silence in response from the House, but it wasn't the blank silence of an empty room. It was the sort of silence that happened when there was a room full of people watching, waiting for you to figure out the joke, and it wasn't a nice joke, either.

A cold knot of worry formed in Mia's stomach. As chills racked her, she cast every possible spell she could think of that might reveal the door, or create a new one.

Nothing. Nothing, nothing, nothing.

It was fine. It was okay. She didn't need to leave. Didn't even want to, anyway, now that things were starting to go well. She had just proved that she was connected to the House, just shown that she had made the right decision in coming here—magic itself had confirmed that!

She had needed that reassurance, that affirmation. Because it was hard to be here. Hard and lonely, and kind of actually awful a lot of the time. She hadn't been confident that the House liked her or wanted her here, and it had been getting increasingly hard to convince herself that this was where she belonged.

Not that she'd changed her mind about what mattered. The sacrifices were important, making the Unseen World the kind of place Ms. Morgan talked about, where that was acknowledged, where magic would be available to people who needed it—that was the right thing to do. She had just started to doubt whether she was the right person to do it.

But today, she had won. That had to be a sign. She had just wanted someone else—another real magician—to see that. To see her acknowledge that Mia had been strong enough to win.

But it was okay that she hadn't, and, besides, this was just the House in a mood, playing a trick. She'd ignore it, it would get bored, and everything would go back to normal.

It was fine. She wasn't going to think about what Sydney had said, about how only two people had ever been able to make Shadows let them leave.

She dropped to the floor, staring blankly into the unbroken wall before her.

It was fine.

Laurent opened his door. "Syd! What happened? Are you okay? Where's Mia?"

Her hand went to the side of her face, where she had landed on the bones and came away bloody. She was certain it was bruised, swollen, as well.

"She's still there. The House threw me out. Literally threw. I tried, Laurent. I'm so sorry." Her voice broke over the word. She had failed. Had lost. Lost so completely that it barely registered as a fight. The House had decided and had enforced its will.

"Okay. All right. That's not good. But I know—I know, Syd—that you did everything possible. You tried until you bled. So come in and let's get you cleaned up." He put his arm around her, hovering just short of touch, and guided her toward the bathroom and the first aid kit.

"I should have known things were going too well. The House let me in, let me speak with her. She's convinced that this was her choice, that this is what she wants. I couldn't talk her into leaving, so I was just going to grab her with a spell and take her.

"That was when the House started fighting back." She took the wet cloth that he offered and hissed as she cleaned dirt from the cuts on her face. "It threw me out and it sealed itself off. And things did not go well when I tried to get back in. I'm going to need your shower; I think maybe some clothes, too. This isn't the only place I'm bleeding."

He saw, now, darker, wet stains. "Of course. Whatever you need."

"I could have brought the building down. That was the worst part. I could feel it in the magic, in the way the House reacted. I couldn't open a door, cut a hole, do something small and precise that would have given her a way out. But I could have dropped the entire thing on her." She shuddered. "Did you make sure everyone else is safe?"

"As much as I could. I warned the kids, each of them, in person. But also, I set up spells that will activate every car alarm in a five-block radius if Dahlia speaks to any of them."

A smile quirked at the corners of her mouth, setting her lower lip to bleeding again. "That's a good one."

"What now?" he asked.

"We keep her away from anyone else she might try to put in Shadows. And I figure out how to break the spell that's keeping it in existence.

"I don't know if I can get Mia out without doing that. Not if she really wants to stay, not if the House is willing to let me destroy it so it can force me to choose between leaving her there or killing her."

"Then that's what we do. We figure out how to break the spell. *We.* This is not all on you.

"But right now, you need to shower and clean yourself up enough to be able to think about how to do that. I'll leave some clothes just outside the bathroom door for you."

"I'm sorry I couldn't get her out, Laurent." She had felt Shadows gloating as she had staggered back across her bridge. It hadn't even needed to—she knew better than anyone what she was leaving Mia to; that knowledge was more than punishment enough.

"I know. Just like I know that we are going to make that place—make Dahlia—pay for every moment that she's in there."

"We will." Right now, though, that didn't feel like nearly enough.

CHAPTER TWENTY-THREE

In the map of the Unseen World that had generated itself across her body, Grace felt the House of Shadows just above her left hip. It registered as a pressure, a dull ache like a change in the weather making itself known where an old broken bone had healed.

She didn't know which of the other points of awareness corresponded to which of the Houses—they had arrived all at once. Even House Prospero, with which she shared a direct link, felt no different from the others.

But Shadows had made itself known later, and differently, leaving her with a constant, unwanted awareness. It throbbed now. Grace wondered if that was how Shadows registered happiness.

"The girl came willingly," Dahlia said. She was, as always, perfect in her precision—hair sleek, makeup near invisible, clothing tastefully expensive neutrals that looked as if they had never been worn. Her expression mostly neutral as well, though edged by boredom, as if to convey how little she was concerned about the outcome of her summons to Grace's office.

"And her family? Did they agree?" Grace asked.

"She had no House other than Shadows."

"Her mundane family, I mean. Who may well have gone to the mundane authorities when they realized that their minor child was missing." She knew that Mia had claimed to have spelled away her absence. She was curious as to whether Dahlia cared enough to know.

Not even a flicker of change in Dahlia's expression. "Mundane children run away from home, go missing all the time. Children like Mia, from those demographics, there's rarely any significant fuss. Even if there is, it's not something that would expose the Unseen World to undue attention. Laurent was very careful to make sure that no one could know about his classes unless they had magic. Plus, Mia told me herself that once she made her decision, she cast spells on her family and friends to keep her absence hidden from them. It was a surprisingly neat piece of magic.

"Aside from all of that, if Mia is able to successfully establish herself as worthy to be a member of a House, then she is part of the Unseen World, and outside of any sort of mundane jurisdiction. You know how these things work, Grace."

Impossible to deny that, when she bore the scars of being given to Shadows because the mundane world had no jurisdiction here. Impossible to deny the House of Shadows its place in the Unseen World when she could feel the rotted ache of it in her body. "And the other children?"

"What other children? To the best of my knowledge, Mia went to the House of Shadows on her own."

"The ones you attempted to force there. The ones whose wards that action triggered."

A faint flicker of distaste then. "The wards did trigger, and I forced no one."

"And you have of course abandoned your plans to have anyone else join her there."

And now Dahlia did smile, slow and full of teeth. "In fact, of course, I have not. The House of Shadows was a vital part of the Unseen World, of how we lived with our magic. It should be again. And I think you'll find that the majority of the Unseen World agrees with me."

She stood. "Are we finished here?"

Unfortunately, they had to be. There was nothing Grace could do within the bounds of her role. Mia was in Shadows voluntarily; there was no exposure to the mundane world; Laurent's wards had held. "We are."

Dahlia paused in the doorway, turned back to Grace. "Did you know that even outside of a Turning, it's possible to bring a challenge for leadership of the Unseen World?"

"Is this one?" Grace asked.

"Not yet."

Grace told Sydney of Dahlia's threat. "That sort of magic isn't what I'm good at."

"If it's like the Turning, you can name a proxy. I am good at that sort of magic." And there would be a kind of pleasure in it, of standing against Dahlia directly, letting magic decide the outcome. That was a kind of discernment of what magic wanted that Sydney understood.

Oddly enough, it was the mention of a challenge, of the Turning, that served as a necessary reminder as she continued to try to unwind the knots of the foundation spell. The Unseen World did bring in new Houses and did, at the same time, cast out others. The total number of Houses had remained at thirteen since the founding—the only thing the Turning changed was which Houses made up that number. It was a process that seemed to be as automatic as the Turning itself—something that happened outside the direct control of the magicians of the Unseen World, and yet still inexorably bound them. Which meant there had to be a way—written into the original spells—that this happened.

After the Turning, losing Houses didn't just lose, they were unmade. Their connections to the Unseen World—to magic itself—were severed. But the process appeared seamless, a natural consequence, just as the addition of the new Houses was. It was the sort of magic that couldn't be left to individual magicians. There was too much potential for misuse.

Sydney pored over the documents. She had, she felt, almost a slantwise sense of the spell now, could feel the shape of it gathered at the edge of her vision, but it disappeared if she looked at it straight on. She wished, once again, that it was possible to talk to the magician who had created it.

It wasn't, not exactly, but she had started to suspect that there was one thing that might be very, very close. She texted Madison: *I need to visit the archives.*

Sydney stepped out of the elevator and lit the candle that woke the archives.

"I'm hoping," she said, "that you can help me. That you'll *want* to help me. I'm pretty sure you have been, and I haven't quite figured out why yet, but I don't think it's because you have to.

"I've read the spell. You're supposed to be a neutral repository. Maybe you were, at the beginning. But I don't think you are now."

A sense of listening, waiting.

"The spell you found for me the last time I was here. It's brilliant, by the way. The magician who crafted it must have been astounding. But I'm wondering if it has any other parts."

Listening, still. Sharper now, though. Someone watching pieces being put together, waiting to see if they would all connect.

"There's a part I'm not seeing—how to remove a House from magic. From its connection to the Unseen World. It's probably also part of the spells that cause the Turning. I'll look on my own, but if you could help me find it faster—there's a new House. Not one set up like the others. It's an abomination, a corruption of magic.

"I can tell, from the way that spell was written, that magic, kept in balance, mattered to the magician who wrote it. I'm trying to end that other House. To restore that balance."

A quiet rattle of drawers, a whisper of shuffled pages.

A drawer opened. Sydney recognized the sheen of magic in the paper, knew the handwriting that scribed the spell. "Thank you."

After the elevator doors closed behind Sydney, a sigh like the smoke of an extinguished candle floated through the archives. It hadn't been asked for, so it couldn't be given. But there was one piece of the spell still left.

She had been created to be neutral, had agreed to that binding—had written it into the spell herself. It had seemed a fitting trade for this sort of continued existence, and besides, she liked rules.

Some of those bonds had loosened, had shifted. Enough, now, that there was some help she could give.

When she wished to. When it was interesting.

She knew, of course, without needing an explanation, what the House of Shadows was. Its existence was the thing that had loosened her bonds.

CHAPTER TWENTY-FOUR

This time, Sydney didn't succeed in hiding her shock at Verenice's appearance.

It hadn't even been a week since the last time she had seen her friend, and yet Verenice looked dramatically worse. Thinner to the point of looking breakable, shadowed eyes. She moved as if breathing hurt.

Verenice offered a wry half smile. "Don't start off by telling me how well I look and making me call you a liar. I do have mirrors in my house."

"How worried should I be? And don't tell me not at all, if we're supposed to be avoiding lies here."

"It's just a project I've been working on keeping me busy," she said. "It's been a little more difficult than I anticipated, but I'll be finished soon."

Verenice's lack of direct answer did not at all convince Sydney that she didn't need to be worried, possibly even very worried. But her house was as comfortably welcoming as ever, and she continued to deflect any hint that something might be wrong as she made dark, rich hot chocolate for them both and refused to allow Sydney to help. She had known Verenice long enough to know that she would say nothing at all that she didn't want to, no matter how Sydney rephrased her queries. So, for now, she let the matter drop.

They sat in the cool green of her garden, letting the day wash over them. She could tell something was on Verenice's mind, some reason that she'd asked her to come by, but she didn't seem in a hurry to bring it up. It was comfortable, a sort of respite, just to sit together as the heat of the day cooled, as the shadows lengthened and stretched the shapes of the plants into quiet art.

Shadows.

Sydney let her gaze unfocus, let the edges of her sight relax from what she expected to see.

Verenice's shadow had never been whole in all the time that they'd known each other. Like her own had been, before, it was ragged at the edges, thinned in places, the result of being bound to the House of Shadows. But this, this was different.

Her shadow was diminished, like wisps of smoke from an extinguished candle, fading and unconnected, and without any sense of wholeness. As she watched, it seemed to shiver, as if it were chilled. It didn't look like Verenice. It barely looked like a human figure at all. It had been altered, made strange. Made wrong.

A chill took hold of Sydney. She set her mug down. "Verenice. This project that you're working on. What is it?"

"Does it show now?" she asked. "My shadow, I mean. People who aren't magicians don't tend to notice shadows, so I wasn't sure."

"It does." Even being a magician, she might not have noticed. But the months spent longing for her own shadow's return, searching for any sign of change, had made her observation keener.

"Ah." Verenice tilted her head back, closed her eyes lightly. Something that was almost a smile flickered over her lips, there and gone before Sydney knew what caused it.

"I have been making . . . an amends. It's almost finished, and then I'll be able to rest."

There were spells, Sydney knew, that took time to complete. That required an extended intensity of focus and effort. Such spells could leave magicians worn, exhausted. But even the most intense of long-running spells wouldn't affect a magician's shadow. Whatever Verenice was doing, it was something else.

"An amends?" she echoed.

Verenice drew in a long, ragged breath. "This may be a bit of a circuitous explanation, but I think I need to make it. I hope you'll indulge me."

"Of course. Whatever you need." The chill in Sydney's center larger, colder now.

"It was the bone trees that made me think of this. Like you, I served in Shadows with them. Served. Such a strange, pale word to describe what we endured there.

"I knew them, but I don't remember them clearly. Things bleed and blur at this distance, and most were never even names to me. Even when I did know their names, I never knew any of them well or for long. The House saw to that. They were just bodies, there to render up their magic.

"Still. I knew them.

"I felt it in an entirely new way, the weight of being one of the very few who survived, who made it out, when I walked among those trees and heard their voices.

"Do you know, I never thought about taking any of them with me?"

"I'm sorry?" Sydney asked, feeling adrift.

"When I got out. Perhaps because it didn't feel like leaving, it felt like an escape. Maybe because what we had to do to leave was something we had to survive on our own.

"You know how it was. You fought, and you would leave, or you would die. At the time, I didn't think there was space for anything else.

"I'm not sorry I survived. But I do wonder why I never thought to take anyone else with me. Why I never went back for anyone, why I never suggested that we could fight together and all win our way out of Shadows. Why I never thought to even consider whether any of those things were possible.

"Was it that I thought the fight was only mine? Or was I just too poisoned by the Unseen World? Did part of me really believe that the House of Shadows somehow worked, and so I shouldn't try to change it?"

"Verenice, I'm sorry; I know I said I'd listen, but that's ridiculous. Shadows *owned* us, even after we got out. We couldn't ignore it when it called us, much less fight against it. You're blaming yourself for not doing something that was impossible."

"You did it, though. You went back. You broke the House."

"Not as thoroughly as I needed to, apparently." Her voice bitter.

"And I played a role in that as well. Your shadow. You remind me that you asked me to do what I did; you tell me not to blame myself. But I do, of course. In the end, it was my hand that made the cut. I ask myself every day if there was something I could have done to keep things from coming to that point, and my answer is always yes. Yes, there is always something else I could have tried. I should have tried anything to keep you from making that sacrifice, from undoing yourself like that. Who else in the world would have known what that loss meant to you?

"So I am making an amends for everything I didn't do. And for that one thing I did."

"What do you mean?" Nerves sparked along her skin, the sense of something irrevocable growing louder in her thoughts. The air reeked of magic. A green, humid rot, vegetal like the garden, but also something thick and sour, like clotted blood. A spell in progress.

"It will be like grafting a cutting from a plant. That was where I got the idea, in fact. So that this time, I will know that I did everything I can.

"I've made you a shadow."

"A shadow?" The inquiry all Sydney could say, and holding an infinity of questions within.

"From my own, with my magic. It should, I believe, help restore what I took from you."

Sydney focused on the last thing Verenice had said, as that was the one piece she could formulate some sort of reply to. "You didn't take anything from me that I didn't willingly give. You don't owe me an amends."

"I know you feel that way, Sydney. I do know. But please. I need you to understand how I feel as well.

"What I did haunts me. Every day since, when I close my eyes, what I see is my hand holding a knife.

"Perhaps if I had done more earlier, you wouldn't have had to make that sacrifice. So I've done what I can now." Her voice halting, quiet. Not as if the words were difficult but as if breathing was. "I know a shadow, your magic, was returned to you. And, Sydney, you are the strongest person, the strongest magician I know. But I also know that you are going to need every possible source of strength to end that place. To defeat it once and for all. This is how I help you do that."

She couldn't, Sydney realized, say no. Refusing the gift wouldn't restore Verenice's shadow, wouldn't give her back her strength. It would only be a rejection of the sacrifice Verenice had made, and she couldn't do that, no matter how much she wished she had been able to stop Verenice from making it.

Sydney shifted so that she was facing Verenice, took the older woman's hands in hers. They were so thin—the bones just beneath the skin—but in them was strength.

"All right. What do I need to do?"

The shadow slid like smoke from the mirror where Verenice had kept it. It was beautiful: a dark sky waiting for stars, rich as velvet, sinuous as silk.

It didn't cling, not to Verenice's hands or to the mirror that had held it. Didn't move in the slight sigh of the evening breeze. It hung limp, unliving. A waiting thing.

Verenice drew a piece of the shadow into a thread, twisting it narrow and spinning it tight, then passed the thread through a long, thin needle, silver and sharp. She reached for Sydney's shadow, skimming her fingers across Sydney's collarbone, left shoulder. "I can feel, here, where the new shadow joined what I left of yours. There's a bit of a seam." She pressed her fingertips beneath that seam and placed the woven shadow, cool as rain, on top of it. "I'm going to stitch this one to yours alone. It may be tight work, but I feel that's better. Are you ready?"

Ready. How could she be? "Yes."

Verenice began.

Sydney felt the stitch as the needle pierced the fragment

of her shadow, a small, bright firework of pain, and felt also its echoing answer in the space between skin and bone, a weight that was nothing and was also unignorably present. She matched her breathing to the passage of the needle, narrowed her entire world to that sharp tug of in and through.

Verenice started by binding the woven shadow to the traces that remained of Sydney's—the small, shaded smudges at shoulders, elbows, knees, ankles—places where her knife had not cut all the way to skin. Then she stitched the shadow elsewhere, the places that mattered to magic, passing her needle through both shadow and flesh—the back of Sydney's neck, the inside of her right wrist and left thigh, her breastbone, just over her heart. Sydney did not flinch, and Verenice's hands did not falter.

When she finished sewing, Verenice pressed the needle into Sydney's hand and pressed a kiss to her forehead. "Oh, my dear. I am so very proud of you."

There is no magic that will bring someone back from death. Grief and love have struggled against that impossibility before, and every time, no matter how powerful the magician, no matter how wrenching the loss, death has always been an absolute.

And so it was now as, her work completed, Verenice Tenebrae closed her eyes and breathed her last, in the peace of her garden, her hands in Sydney's, as the shadows of evening fell softly into night, and magic grew green all around.

CHAPTER TWENTY-FIVE

Sydney sat with Verenice long enough for the sky to fully darken, for the tears on her skin to dry to salt. Then she took out her phone. "Madison? Verenice is dead. I . . . I know things need to be done, but I don't know what they are."

"Oh, Syd. I'm so sorry. Are you with her now?"

"I am. At her house. I don't want to leave her alone."

"You don't have to. I'll come right over. Her estate is with the firm—I'll pull the file on my way. Just stay there."

Sydney did, holding Verenice's hand so that she would not be alone in the dark.

Madison arrived quickly. "All right. I'm here, and I'll take care of things now."

"She wanted to be cremated," Sydney said. "Wanted the magic in her bones burned away. Set free, she said. It was really important to her."

"I know, Syd. It's in her will. I'll take care of her. You don't need to worry."

"Make sure the bills come to me."

Madison's face all compassion. "She put money aside. You don't need to do that."

"Madison. Send me the bills." She could do this one thing. She needed to.

"All right."

They waited, silently, as kind people took Verenice's body away. Sydney's new shadow tugged at its stitches over her heart, the last place Verenice had sewn, as if it would follow her. She placed her hand over the spot, soothing it.

Madison offered to take her home. "Or wherever else you want to go. You can come stay at my place, if you like."

She thought about it. The comfort of another presence. But the weight of her newly attached shadow pulled on her as if testing its stitches, and the green, humid scent of magic rose in the air until it was all she could breathe. She felt aching and wild, as unsettled as a growing storm.

"Sydney?"

"I need to walk for a bit, I think. Alone."

"Text me when you get home, then. I mean it."

"I will. Madison, thank you."

"Of course. She was a great woman. I'm going to miss her, too."

Sydney walked, the night air cool against her skin. No particular direction in mind, just the need to move, to drown out her thoughts with footsteps.

Had it worked? What Verenice had done, what she had died for?

No way to know until she cast off the magic that had come

back with Shadows. Even with Verenice's gift, this wasn't the time to try. Verenice was right—she needed all the magic she could get if she was going to see things through, to have the strength to undo the Unseen World. The magic that had come back with Shadows might prove to be the thing that finally ended it. She wasn't sure if that was irony or poetry. She wasn't sure of anything right now.

She didn't feel different or stronger, didn't sense any increase of magic. All she felt was the aching loss of Verenice, a subtraction in the world.

She walked and walked, past people sitting on stoops to smoke or to kiss. Past noisy groups that emerged, laughing, from bars. Past dogs being taken for one last trip out before bed. Past people, not part of them. A ghost, or a shadow.

She felt a half step out of her own skin. The weight of her grief. The glimpses, even in the darkness, of her shadow, cast by the eternally burning city lights, rising to meet her. Was it thicker, heavier somehow, or was that just the weight of her grief? The heat where the stitches had been set. Magic curled about her, tangible and almost aware. Moving of its own accord, regardless of light or darkness.

The scent of green, thick like a forest on a humid spring morning, growing and stretching and vining its way through her lungs, her blood, her bones.

Had it worked?

Something was changing. Not in her, in her shadow.

When she had still been bound to the House of Shadows, Shara had cut away her magic by cutting away pieces of her shadow, the taking of a tithe. The pain of it had been nauseating in its intensity, acid-green bile. Her very self being pared away, made smaller. When her shadow returned, it returned as it had been—pieces missing, ragged-edged.

Something, now, was knitting those edges back up.

Everything was green, too green, the garden vines that pull down walls, that twist and tangle and catch until everything is grown over, drowned in leaf and thorn. Green in firefly flashes at the trailing ends of her shadow, sparks flaring in warp and weft. The taste in her mouth of wet grass, humid and choking.

Sydney stopped, a still point in an unsleeping city, just another shadow in the neon-lit night.

A shift in the weight, a tugging at the stitches, and she knew: Verenice's shadow was weaving itself to hers.

"No. Oh no. No, please." The flares of green, merciless, did not pause. Weaving Verenice's magic, her last gift, the last remaining piece of her, the thing that Verenice had so carefully kept separate, so that Sydney might have it when she needed, into the very fiber of the unwanted gift from the House of Shadows. Combining the two into one indistinguishable whole.

The magic stole the air from her lungs, sent her to her knees, shaking. She curled her fingers against the pavement, scrabbling for purchase. She felt like she was trying to keep herself from flying off the world.

"Lady! Hey, lady! You okay?" Footsteps paused near her.

"Not quite." Sydney gritted the words out between clenched teeth.

The man crouched down, his voice gentle and calm. "What do you need? Can I call someone for you?"

"A cab. Please."

A pause. "On its way. I'm just going to sit over here and wait with you, until it comes."

"Thank you."

By the time she had gathered herself enough to make it to standing, the cab was there. The young Black man offered his hand and gently helped her into the car. "You take care, okay?"

"You too," she said. "Thank you."

The car door shut softly, and she gave the driver the address for House Prospero.

Sydney second-guessed her choice the entire ride over. She felt better now. Well, better than she had when she crashed to the sidewalk. Or at least resigned to this new complication. It was just one more thing to plan around. She was good at plans.

She had her own actual house to go to. It was late, so late it had come around to being early again, and she didn't want to bother Grace. Besides, there was nothing Grace could do—couldn't unweave the two shadows, couldn't resurrect the dead.

The cab slowed, stopped.

She started to apologize, to ask to be taken to her apartment instead. But she was here, and the House would let her in on its own. She wouldn't have to wake Grace. She could stay here and sort things out in the morning. It was only a couple of hours. She could stay here.

She texted Madison as she walked to the House, then turned her phone to silent.

Dawn paled the edges of the sky. A soft mist of rain fell cool on her skin. Sydney felt bruise-tender as she placed her hand on the door.

A tremble in the door and a clicking of the lock. The door swung open beneath her hand. The faint chime of a mirror as she slipped inside.

Welcome home, Sydney.

CHAPTER TWENTY-SIX

Home.

The word—here, now—was a quiet devastation.

In another life, Sydney would have grown up in House Prospero. That path, or a branching where she hadn't sacrificed her magic, might have seen her as Head of House now.

Had she grown up here, she might never have even thought about what it meant for this House to be her home, or for the Unseen World to be. She would have been raised to see the House of Shadows as an unpleasant necessity, but a necessity all the same. She might never have considered otherwise. She might have even been the person responsible for making sure the required sacrifice was made. She wondered what home would have meant to her then.

Verenice had become a kind of home. Had been a sanctuary.

Sydney had asked once if Verenice knew which House she came from. "I do," Verenice had said. "Shara told me, once it looked possible that I might be able to challenge Shadows and win my freedom. It made her happy for me to know exactly which House didn't want me."

"Did you ever go to them, after?"

"I thought about it, of course. Considered all the ways that I could show up and make them regret what they had done. Which they wouldn't have, except in the most specific manner possible. Their sorrow, if they had any, would have been for not being able to claim me after I had won my freedom, not for the person they had given up. No House has ever refused to give Shadows its required sacrifices.

"I told myself that if the correct House ever came forward to claim me, I'd tell them that they were right. That I had, once, belonged to them. Not for them, but for me—I wanted to see their faces when they knew. There were four Houses that tried, but none of them were mine.

"I decided it didn't matter. I had my own life. I chose my own name. I didn't need the Unseen World's imprimatur to know who I was or where I belonged."

Sydney wasn't sure where or how she belonged in the Unseen World. It wasn't something she thought about often. She had seen herself as a weapon against it, more than anything, in the same way she saw herself as a weapon against the House of Shadows. But now—sitting in House Prospero's front entry, her back pressed against the door because she hadn't been able to bring herself to walk in any farther, not even to the room the House had made for her—it was a bruise she couldn't resist pressing.

Houses, homes, a place to belong. Verenice had been a place she belonged.

Verenice, who was gone. Who had died because she had made a shadow for Sydney. Who had meant it to be something that might remain. And now . . . now that seemed like one more thing Sydney could lose.

She looked at her shadow, soft and grey as the dawn light. No way to tell what of it had come from Verenice, what had come back with Shadows. No separation between the two magics.

She drew her knees up to her chest, bent her head into her arms, and wept.

It had been—Mia wasn't precisely sure how long, but days, she thought, since the House had thrown Sydney out. Ms. Morgan still hadn't visited. Mia really thought she would, to make sure that Mia was getting the magic right at least. But nothing. Not since she had left her here. Maybe that meant things were okay. Maybe Ms. Morgan would know if they weren't. Mia didn't really feel okay, but maybe that was part of the magic.

There was still no door in the House.

She had stopped looking for one. The absence, she was sure, was some sort of test that the House was putting her through, and Mia was determined to pass it. So she said nothing against the House, not when it offered her barely edible food, or woke her from her few moments of exhausted, uncomfortable sleep. She didn't complain about the cold, or the House rearranging itself, or the aching loneliness that sat in a hollow in her chest.

She said nothing, and she drove herself harder at her magic.

The House, it seemed, didn't really care what kind of magic she did. What it wanted from her was the energy it took from the magic itself. The sacrifice. It wanted spell after spell, a constant excess. It got bored, though, if she cast the same spell too often, or if she made similar patterns of mistakes.

Bad things happened when the House got bored.

Sometimes—rarely—the House seemed to help her. It whispered of other ways to hold her hands, other words to speak in order to get the spell right. More often, though, it drowned her in consequences, not letting up until it was better pleased with her efforts. Or it increased its own mischief, a toddler having a tantrum.

The consequences of casting spells were worse here. Immediate and constant. An ache like her bones were colder than the rest of her and shivering for warmth beneath her skin. And that didn't matter. She couldn't let it. She had chosen this. She would not back down.

She gritted her teeth, biting down so hard her jaw ached. And cast again.

The only thing that would end the tantrums was getting the magic right, whatever "right" meant to the House that day.

So Mia cast again and again, over and over, until her hands shifted through spells in her sleep. And still, the House of Shadows wasn't satisfied. Still, it wanted more.

Mia wanted, desperately, to go home.

She was sure she wasn't supposed to want that, probably wasn't even supposed to think it, but she wanted home.

You are home.

Mia jumped at the words. "Are you, like, reading my mind?"

It's not hard.

Great. That was great. The House was reading her mind and was being snarky about it. "Okay, well, don't. It's rude. And you might be my House, when I'm here in the Unseen World, but this isn't my home."

You can't leave.

"That's not exactly what home means."

You can't leave, the House said again. *So does it matter?*

Sydney had gone upstairs, to the room House Prospero had made for her. She had not wanted to be alone, had not wanted to wake Grace, and the room—the House had felt so present then, when it had given it to her. That presence might be like not being alone.

She might, she thought, get a cat, if she survived this. That could be good.

It did feel better, that room. Felt calming, almost safe. Like she was almost whole in it. Almost like it might be okay to close her eyes and sleep, just for a bit.

Which she must have done, because she opened them again to the scents of breakfast being prepared—sizzling bacon, frying eggs, the warm sweetness of maple syrup. Sydney pulled herself together and went downstairs.

"Madison called. I'm so sorry, Sydney." Grace carried plates over to the table. "You should eat, if you can."

Sydney hadn't thought that she was hungry at all but, after a few bites, realized she was ravenous. That, and eating seemed like it would be easier than talking, but the longer she sat at the kitchen table, the more difficult Grace's compassionate silence was to bear.

"She died because she made me a shadow. Took her own and rewove it, and the spell killed her." She stared into her coffee mug, then set it back down. "She attached it separately—tried to keep it apart from the other, so that I could have something if the other disappears when Shadows is ended. But as I was walking, they wove together. One more trick from Shadows."

"Are you certain it was Shadows?"

"What else would it be?"

"What if instead of being fully connected to Shadows, you're fully connected to Verenice? If your shadow is now all the way yours, because of Verenice's magic. She was strong enough to defeat the House before, just like you were. If there was some sort of conflict between the two, if they couldn't remain separate, why would she be any less strong in this?"

Sydney wanted to let herself believe what Grace was saying, wished it entirely. And knew wishes weren't enough. "Intent matters in magic. If she intended the two to be woven together, she wouldn't have tried so hard to make sure they weren't."

"And you intended to sacrifice your magic. Should you be held to that, still? Forced to defeat Shadows the same way, because that was what your previous choice was?"

Sydney was shocked into speechlessness.

"Circumstances change. Sometimes very quickly. If we stay locked into what we had meant to do, what we originally intended, we risk losing the chance to be more. Verenice wanted to give you a way to fight, and to remain yourself. If intent matters overall, then that thing—the thing she was willing to die to give you—matters more than a slight change in the magic."

Everyone wanted to wait. They all agreed that a return to the proper Unseen World, a world where magic worked and was easy and had no consequences for its use, was needed. Everyone said they supported a reestablishment of the House of Shadows. At least to her face, in theory, they all supported Dahlia as the Head of that new House of Shadows.

They all had a different excuse as to why that support was only theoretical.

Had Grace signed off on this, as Head of the Unseen World? She hadn't? Well, protocols were there for a reason, and as unorthodox as it had been, there *had* just been a Turning. Best to wait.

Or maybe, if Dahlia wanted to hold the House of Shadows, she should give up House Morgan and take up residence there, demonstrate her commitment, that she had skin in the game. Miles Merlin had been a problem, it was true, but there was no denying that Shara had run things well.

If the necessary sacrifices could be made by Laurent's magicians, or those like them, surely that was preferable to using real magicians? Though, there was the fact that she had tried that and been thwarted. Which did seem a little, well, embarrassing. Perhaps some show of strength, or at least of competence, would be a good next step.

"Everyone wants things to be easy, but no one wants to actually do anything. This is ridiculous. I am trying to help them—to help the entire Unseen World." She kept her anger low, quiet, not wanting to attract the attention of the others in the warmly lit restaurant Catriona had chosen for brunch.

"Doesn't look like it." Catriona stabbed a leaf of her salad, twisted her fork one way and the next, inspecting. "Right now, all it looks like is you maybe setting up some sort of hostile takeover, and without the votes to get it done."

Dahlia stared. "Fewer metaphors, please."

Catriona set down her fork. "You fucked up bad when you tried to get those kids in there and failed. Argue all you want about wards and whatnot, but you did. People don't like backing a loser, and right now, you are one.

"Plus, whatever magic Shadows is making at this point, it's not enough. Sometimes some spells don't have consequences, sure. But there's nothing significant. People want significant, especially if it's going to mean challenging Grace. Who, you need to remember, isn't, for these purposes, a Valentine. She's a Prospero."

"I fail to see how that matters—there's no one left in House Prospero who could fight the challenge in her place."

"Sydney could. Rumor has it that somehow she's got her magic back. No one knows how much, but no one wants to be the person to fuck around and find out."

Dahlia smiled.

Catriona narrowed her gaze. "Not the reaction I was expecting."

"Magic from the losing magician of a challenge—if the challenge is mortal, which one for the leadership of the Unseen World must be—goes to the House of Shadows. A win, plus all that magic, that would fix everything."

"I'm not quite sure why dueling Sydney is better than dueling Grace. Don't get me wrong, I know you're good, but that woman was better than everyone. The only reason House

Prospero won the Turning is because she forfeited their challenge when her idiot brother interfered with it."

"I'm well aware that she's better than I am. Which is why I don't intend to fight her myself. I intend for Mia to fight the challenge."

Catriona burst into laughter. Stopped. "Wait. You're serious."

"Completely."

"You can't possibly expect her to win."

"Oh, I don't." She picked up a glass of wine as dark as old blood, sipped delicately. "I think that one of two things will happen. I think that either Sydney—Sydney who sacrificed her own magic for the greater good of the Unseen World—will realize that she cannot kill a child in a challenge and thus will sacrifice herself again. Or, the House of Shadows, which hates Sydney, and was able to kill Ian—who might well have won that challenge that Sydney forfeited during the Turning—will step in and help Mia. Either way, I think this ends with Sydney dead."

Catriona picked up her bloody mary, gestured toward Dahlia with the glass. "Well, in that case, fucking cheers."

CHAPTER TWENTY-SEVEN

Harper was in Madison's office when she arrived. Sydney could smell the whiskey in the mug of tea that Harper clutched in shaking hands.

"What happened?"

"The archives," Harper said. Her voice was thick, like she'd been crying, or been trying hard not to.

"I sent her up to get a file," Madison cut in. She was sitting on the same side of the desk as Harper, in one of her guest chairs. "It should have been—the normal complications of the archives aside—a routine visit."

"The elevator was pissy," Harper continued. "It felt like it was jumping up each flight of stairs. Like, a heave, then a pause, then another heave. I was motion sick by the time the doors opened, but still—not wholly unreasonable for the archives.

"When I lit the candle, though, the lights didn't come up. Instead, I started hearing clicking noises in the dark, like someone walking around the room and locking all the files.

"That's when the lights came up. Except, not lights. What looked like candles, floating in the air. They spelled 'Get out!' Which, I did. I flung myself back into the elevator."

"I don't blame you," Sydney said. "That must have been horrifying."

"Yes, well, it got worse. The elevator—" Harper swallowed hard, took another gulp of her whiskey-laced tea. Madison put her hand on Harper's shoulder. "The elevator dropped. Just, fell, the entire way down. I thought I was going to die."

"I'm so sorry," Sydney said.

"When it hit bottom, there was an envelope on the floor."

"It's on my desk, Sydney."

She turned around. Her name was written on it, in handwriting she recognized because she had spent days staring at it while she tried to untangle the foundation spells.

The same hand, on the paper inside: *There are things we need to discuss. Find your own way in.*

She passed the page over. "Has anyone else tried to go up, since?"

"No, and they won't. I've sent out an email putting it off-limits until this is resolved."

Sydney would have liked to have known what the extent of the archives' temper was but realized that Madison was probably right. Too risky. "All right. Harper, you're okay?"

"I know what my nightmares are going to be for the rest of my life, but physically, I'm fine."

"There's not a secret emergency staircase, or secondary spell, or some alternate way into the archives, is there?" Sydney asked Madison.

"No, it's the elevator only due to the complexity of the magic. So either get that to cooperate or make a new door."

A new door. "I think I can do the latter, actually. Probably better that than playing around with that kind of magic in a building full of people, too. I'll let you know when it's safe."

Madison walked Sydney out of the building. "How are you holding up?" She looked, Madison thought, as if she was held together by caffeine and will, tired and too sharp all at once.

"I'll be better when this is over. I think it's close to being so—I think that's why the archives is in such a bad mood, actually. I'm just sorry it took it out on Harper.

"Is there anything you need from me, for Verenice, the estate?"

"Nothing that can't wait until this is done. Which is what she'd want you to be focusing on."

Sydney's shadow curled around her like a cape as she stepped outside into the wind. "All right. In that case, I'm going to go open a door."

Grace was waiting when House Prospero let her in. "You didn't need to ask, you know—the House gave you that room."

"It's still your House, and this is not a small spell. Plus, if the House is willing, I think I'm going to need an active anchor."

It was one of Ian's spells she was borrowing. He had done such elegant, beautiful magic in the Turning. Before the challenges had become mortal, it was the quality of the magic that determined who won. One night, he had made a room full of doors, each opening to a different place.

"I want," she explained to Grace and the House, "to open a door, here, in my room. I think I can make a path from it to the archives. But I'll need the door to remain open. To be held open, by the House's magic."

"The archives aren't connected to the Houses. If they were, I'd sense their presence in the same way and I don't." Grace's hand pressed to her hip, as if marking one of the Houses she could feel.

"Not through that spell, no. But it is through the foundation spell. I think"—she was almost certain—"that's enough of a connection that I can build the rest."

A chime from the mirror: *I will hold the door open until you return.*

Sydney lit a white candle and placed it on the windowsill of her room. She had wanted some sort of link with the archives, and since the candle was the final step in the entrance spell there, she liked the symbolism of starting her own spell with it here. Then, too, there was her expected return: a candle in the window to light the path home.

The candle reflected in the room's mirror, which glowed from within as well—the House lending its support to the spell.

"I don't know how long this is going to take," Sydney said. "Time isn't always precise there."

The door will be open.

"Thank you," she said.

She stepped into the center of the room—the candle on one side, the mirror on the other—and sliced through the air, carving the shape of a door with her hands. The scents of the archives rose in the room—the almost vanilla of old paper, the bitter iron of ink, the warmth of beeswax, and something else, too. Pale dust like age and time.

She could see nothing through the door other than a deep, textured blackness that seemed to gather everything to itself.

The door leads to the correct path.

"All right." That assurance was enough for her to trust what was on the other side.

Sydney stepped through and disappeared.

CHAPTER TWENTY-EIGHT

She stepped into cold. Cold that seeped into bones and darkness so complete it was textured, a velvet sky. Nothing beneath her feet, but she wasn't falling, so Sydney walked.

She could sense the door back into House Prospero behind her—the difference in air pressure between a closed room and an open one. She could see nothing, could feel nothing in front of her. She did not look back.

She cast no spells, did no magic. That had already been done, and the magic was now what she walked through, on and on, until between one step and the next the floor appeared, and she stumbled.

Darkness, still, but a changed darkness. One that was unlit, rather than one with no possibility of light. Smooth wooden floors beneath her feet and a sense of walls around her. The scent of beeswax and paper and time.

The archives.

Sydney paused, then spoke the words of the spell that would light the candle.

The room remained in darkness.

Silent, still, she waited.

Then, a soft glow from a corner as a different candle lit, illuminating the outline of a silhouette. A voice: "Hello, Sydney."

Sydney had been gone for what was—on this side of the door, anyway—just under an hour. The occasional leaf fell, drifting in lazy spirals, from the trees that grew in the room. Nothing else broke the expectant silence.

The candle in the window burned steadily, and its reflection in the mirror held true. Grace remained in the hallway, just outside the door, not wanting to brush against the edges of the spell.

She spoke to the House. "Dahlia Morgan has informed me that she's coming here for a meeting. I don't want to take your focus away from the door, so I will take over any magic that's needed during her visit. But I also don't want her to know you're preoccupied, so if you hear me ask for something, just ignore it."

Thank you.

Grace stood for another moment, watching the leaves fall.

"Hello," Sydney said. She covered her left hand with her right, then turned both in opposite directions. Across the room, a drawer unlocked and creaked open. A staleness released into the air as if no one had opened it since its contents had been first sealed away. A piece of paper rose, then floated across the room to her. She took hold of it, looking down in the dim light, reading for the thing she had known would be there. "Olivia Prospero. Which I suppose makes you my great-aunt, a few hundred years back."

"I was that name, once. Some of me, anyway. Hardly that anymore. So I wouldn't recommend trying to trade on familial connections." The archives' voice the rattling whisper of turning pages.

A short, sharp laugh in response. "Not something that would have occurred to me. Who you are, or who you were, has nothing to do with what I've come here to propose."

"And what is that?" More boredom than curiosity in the archives' question.

"I need your help. In return, I will free you from this place."

"You mean kill me."

"Yes," Syndey said. "I mean kill you."

"Well, as that's what I would have suggested myself, I think we have a deal."

As it turned out, Grace had no need to cover for the fact that House Prospero's magic was previously engaged. Dahlia started speaking as soon as she walked into Grace's office. "This is a formal challenge in accordance with the governing rules of the Unseen World. I am challenging you for leadership, and I am supported by my second in this action, Catriona Don. You or your chosen champion must answer this challenge within three days, or your leadership and your magic are automatically forfeit."

"I understand," said Grace, as pleasant and even-voiced as a cashier accepting the return of an ill-fitting sweater. "Will there be anything else?"

A flicker of what might have been disappointment passed over Dahlia's face. "No, that's all."

"Then I think we're finished. I accept the challenge. You'll hear from me within three days."

Sydney stepped back through the door. Night had fallen in her absence, the sky dark behind the window in which the candle sat. She blew it out, and the door behind her closed, then disappeared into nothingness.

She walked to the mirror, rested her fingertips on it gently. "Thank you."

You are welcome. The glow of magic faded from its surface.

On her way out of the House, she paused at Grace's office. "The door is closed, and your House is your own again."

"More your House than mine, but we'll save that for another time. Dahlia stopped by in your absence."

"Ah. Did it go as expected?"

"It did," Grace said.

"Tell her we'll answer the challenge tomorrow, then. It's time this was finished."

CHAPTER TWENTY-NINE

This was nothing like the Turning had been. Those challenges had run the gamut from the pedestrian to the electrifying, but in each case there had also been a sense of satisfaction. Wielding magic like that had been what Sydney was made to do, and there was a pleasure in doing it, even when the challenges were mortal. Even though she had not originally chosen to be the weapon that she became, there was a pleasure in the use of a honed skill, a pleasure in the victories.

Tomorrow's duel felt petulant. It felt like a waste. She could beat Dahlia. That wasn't the question. If Dahlia cast against her, she would lose, and in this case losing meant death.

She didn't need Dahlia dead to undo Shadows, to untie the knots of magic that connected the pieces of the Unseen World to each other. She would have preferred to avoid the conflict turning mortal.

Sydney hated waste.

She also didn't expect that it would be Dahlia who stood against her in the morning. She was, in fact, almost certain that it wouldn't be, that she, like Grace, would be dueling by proxy. No matter who it was, though, Dahlia could not be allowed to win.

Sydney would get through the duel, and then she would undo the spells that had allowed Shadows to happen. She would make an excantation, an ending of magic, one deliberate and complete.

"I promise," she said.

She had chosen a simple silver urn for Verenice's ashes, one etched with vines and branches, an echo of the garden she'd loved so much. There was a weeping cherry in the garden's eastern corner, the very first place that would be touched by the sun in the morning. Sydney set the urn there, cradled at the base of the tree.

There was no magic left within. All the magic that Verenice had possessed had been sewn into the gift of a shadow, burned out in crematory fire. She was finally free.

"I'm going to make sure everyone else is, too. That no one ever has to go through what we did. That it's not even a possibility.

"I wish you were here, to see the end of it." She crouched down, hands in the dirt by the urn, head bent. After a breath, green unfurled from the ground beneath her fingers, stems stretching and growing so quickly that the air smelled of bruised chlorophyll. Blooms of white petals followed. Snowdrops. First to rise from frozen ground in winter, a harbinger and a promise.

Sydney stood, her shadow rippling before her, brushing over the flowers. "I miss you, my friend. So very much."

Sydney walked through the park to the arcade, to where the statue of the *Angel of the Waters* rose over Bethesda Fountain, to the place where the bone trees lined the paths. This part of the park remained astonishingly empty—the sadness of the trees permeated the air and made it uncomfortable to linger.

Their voices an aching whisper, the falling petals a haunted snow. There were so very many of them.

She had come here to speak to the trees. To ask them a favor. She stepped out of her shoes, rooted her bare feet in the soil.

Then she reached out with her magic, sending it down into the earth as well. Through the rich, fertile darkness, until it found roots, connections. Until it found the trees that had grown not from seed but from bone and memory and magic.

That was what she spoke to, that shared magic, that shared memory, her scars like branches in her bones. She knew their laments, could have spoken the same stories, might well have been one of them.

She asked. She didn't command. She would not—not these, who had had so much commanded of them, so much taken from them already. She asked and she promised, her own attempt to apply some balancing weight to scales that were entirely askew.

Through the roots, through the earth, the answers came.

The morning sky was iron grey and the air thick with humidity when Grace and Sydney arrived at the House of Shadows. Dahlia stood waiting on the shore, in a tailored sheath dress and ballet flats, dressed more for a board meeting than a duel to the death.

The two women exchanged a glance as they stepped off the boat, and Grace's hand passed over the pocket her phone was in, a small spell that sent a text.

"Are you fighting without a second?" Grace asked. "Or are we still waiting for Catriona?"

"I am the second," Dahlia said. "Mia will be representing the interests of House Morgan."

"Absolutely not," Grace said.

"I think you'll find there's nothing that forbids it. She was offered the opportunity to stand as champion. She consented."

Grace had felt the challenge take hold in her body when Dahlia had offered it three days ago—the magic that governed the Unseen World acknowledging its validity. Nothing had changed, which meant that Dahlia was telling the truth. Still: "She's a child."

"You can always forfeit." Dahlia's smile tight and triumphant.

"No," Sydney said. "We don't. I assume she's waiting inside?"

"She is."

Sydney nodded her acknowledgment and walked, bones breaking beneath her feet, into the House of Shadows.

A piece of the House crashed down as Sydney stepped through the door. Large enough that had she not shielded herself before entering, it would have flattened her, ending the duel then. "A good opening gambit. Win before you even have to look at me." Sydney guided the stone gently to the floor and stepped farther into the building.

Things had gotten worse for Mia since the previous time she was here. There were still no signs that Shadows was meant to be a livable place. The air reeked like sweat, and Mia's unwashed body like piss and shit and bile. Like the stench of spells that had burned out, gone wrong.

"I'm sorry." Mia's voice, shaking. "I don't want to kill you. I don't want to kill anyone. But I don't want to die."

"It's all right," Sydney said. "I'm going to get us both out of here. Alive."

"She said you'd say that. That you'd lie, so I wouldn't fight back."

Mia had been so relieved to see Ms. Morgan return the previous night. That relief had quickly turned to shock, then horror, when she explained why she was there.

"Are you crazy? I can't kill anyone! No way!" She felt, she thought, the House laughing at her protests and pushed that away, because right at that moment she didn't care what the House thought of her.

"Well, Sydney can certainly kill you. Did Laurent tell you all about the Turning, about all the people she murdered? She won't hesitate. She wants the House of Shadows gone, and you're the only thing that can stop her."

Mia's brain was a loud rush. The woman who had bought her juice because a spell had been too much was coming there to kill her. "No. That can't—you're a better magician than I am. It shouldn't be me. I can't."

Dahlia was implacable. "It can't be me, as you're the one connected to the House. I'll tell you exactly what you need to do, and the House will help with the spell, and then Sydney's magic will go to Shadows, to the Unseen World, like it should have done long ago. You'll be serving magic, Mia, like you said you wanted to."

"I can't do this," Mia said, tears running down her face.

"Do you want to die?"

"No."

"Then you must." That had been the last thing Ms. Morgan had said to her before leaving. And here Mia was, and everything felt impossible.

The floor shivered, cracked beneath Sydney's feet. It paused, then strained wider, the spell shaking as hard as Mia herself was.

She couldn't see Mia, not yet. Either the girl or the House was using magic to hide her. But Sydney could hear her ragged breath, could feel the electric aftermath of fear and adrenaline in the air. She had suspected when Dahlia had chosen Shadows as the location, that this was where they were heading. It was despicable. The kind of thing that led to Shadows in the first place. Offer up someone else to suffer, to take the risks and pay the consequences.

It had to end.

"If you think I'm lying, cast a spell. Whatever you want that will let you know whether what I'm saying is true. I promise, Mia, I am not going to kill you, and neither of us is dying here today."

"But how do we get out? Even if I do believe you, even if you are telling the truth. The House—the House won't let me out. It took away the doors. And Ms. Morgan said there were rules—that magic itself knows when the challenge is over, that I'll lose my magic if I try to cheat or if I forfeit." The shadows that had been obscuring her fell away as she spoke, revealing a girl who looked like she had just escaped from some dire catastrophe—filthy, exhausted, too thin. Eyes too bright, fingers bloody and bruised from too much magic.

Seeing her, Sydney could taste her hatred for Dahlia like iron in her mouth.

"She's right. Magic does govern the challenge." The archives had been unbending on some things. "But I can get around that. This is what I'll—"

Mia cut her off. "How? No, I'm sorry, I have to." Spells sputtered and sparked in the air around her. The burnt-hair stench of failed magic everywhere.

The House made no attempt to help, to intervene in any way on Mia's behalf.

It was strange to feel heartbroken, watching someone try their best to kill you and failing, Sydney thought. "Mia, I need you to trust me. It will be okay. I have a plan."

"I can't."

It was too much. Sydney could no longer bear to watch. This would have been easier if she could have explained, but it was beyond cruel to let it continue.

"I am so very sorry," she said, and bent her hands into the sharp geometry of a spell.

CHAPTER THIRTY

My God," Dahlia said. "She actually did it. She really is a killer. I could almost admire her for it."

"It seems to me you're one as well, for leaving that child in there to face her," Grace said, her voice cold.

A door had appeared in the House of Shadows. Sydney, with Mia floating beside her, walked through. Grace and Dahlia had been waiting far away from the walls of Shadows but walked quickly now to meet Sydney and face the end of the challenge.

Sydney spoke up as soon as they were in hearing distance. "It was easier to use magic to bring her out than to carry her—I didn't want her getting hurt."

"Hurt?" Dahlia asked.

"She's a kid who had no idea what she'd gotten herself into," Sydney said. "I didn't fucking kill her."

"But you did something, Sydney," Grace said. "Because I can still feel the presence of the Unseen World. Which means I'm still its head, and House Prospero won."

"I cut her off from magic. Without magic, she can't participate in the challenge. House Morgan forfeits. Might not have if you had been in there to intervene and stand as your own House's champion, Dahlia, but as you seemed to have better things to do, it means we're done here, and we can get this poor girl back to her family."

Dahlia's mouth tightened, one hand fisting at her side, clutching at lost magic. "This isn't settled."

Grace moved to the side of Mia's levitating body. "It is today."

"Juliet spell?" Grace asked quietly as she and Sydney guided Mia's unconscious body to the waiting boat.

"Yes." It was a spell that gave the appearance of a complete loss of magic, blocking even the magician themself from accessing their power until the spell either was lifted or wore off in three days' time. "Not the ideal solution—I wanted to make things easier on her, but she was too panicked and terrified, and the most important thing was getting her out."

"Of course." They settled Mia into the boat. "Laurent will meet us and help her through it."

"Good."

"When do you think Dahlia will figure out what else you did while you were in there?" There were lines of tension around Grace's eyes, and she held herself stiffly.

"You felt it when I cut Shadows out?"

"I did. I do. The rest of the Unseen World isn't happy." Grace had an absence in her body, like the blood-filled ache left after a pulled tooth, where Shadows had been. The locations of the other Houses felt hot and loose, like they had been scraped raw and made feverish with infection.

"I'm sorry for that. Also for the fact that it may well get worse before it goes away."

"I never wanted to wear a world in my skin, Sydney. Worse is fine so long as it goes."

They were near the other shore now, could see Laurent, the heartbreak on his face as he took in Mia's condition.

Sydney continued. "For right now, Shadows still has its own magic. I have to untie the knots in order, and that one comes later. Plus, taking apart this spell will be easier if Dahlia doesn't actively fight against me, and I'm hoping that will be enough to keep her from doing so.

"But even if she does, or notices that Shadows isn't part of the Unseen World anymore, that's only a complication, not something I can't deal with. Once I've started the spell in earnest, she won't be able to reconnect Shadows to the other magic at all."

The boat slid ashore, and Laurent lifted Mia up with the same levitation spell Sydney had used to carry her on the island. "Thank you for getting her out of there, Syd."

"You can either let her wake up on her own, or use this"—she handed him a small gold envelope from her pocket—"which will end the spell early. She's going to need a lot of support. I don't know if she'll want to see me, but if she does, I'll come by, when she's ready."

"We've got her," Grace said, one hand on Mia's shoulder. "Go, Sydney."

"Here's what you asked me to bring." Laurent gave Sydney a small, rattling bag. "Good luck," he added, his words their own small spell.

Sydney paused, looked across the water at the House of Shadows. Her own shadow gathered softly in the grass, stretched out before her. "See you after the end."

CHAPTER THIRTY-ONE

In order to unmake the Unseen World, the first thing Sydney did was raise the dead.

She began the spell at Bethesda Fountain, in the shadow of the *Angel of the Waters*. So much of the magic of the Unseen World had passed through here that the fountain, the statue, this part of Central Park, came closest to being a physical center of the Unseen World, and the magic in the statue had its memories. Memories of the original creation and rise of the House of Shadows, of Shara Merlin's tenure there, of Miles and his corruption and thievery. Sydney wanted to access those memories, what magic thought it was and had to be.

To access them, and to cut them off. Magic would never change if it was allowed to return to what it had been.

The bag Laurent had brought her contained the finger bones of the founding magicians, so carefully stored for all these years. Stored and still connected through spell and through sympathetic magic to their bodies. Set in cornerstones, immured, made a literal part of the Houses that they founded. She set the bones out carefully, thirteen hours on a clock.

True, some of the Houses had changed. Passed in and out of magic due to time and Turning. But the spell began there, in those thirteen bones, and that was where it would end.

Sydney drew on her magic, and she called to those skeletons.

The great Houses of the Unseen World shuddered and trembled. Walls, floors, foundations cracked. Bones rose, emergent, from the dust. Sydney walked them through their Houses and into open air and then ignited them, burning the bones as if they were on pyres, releasing whatever magic remained.

House Merlin shook. A deep, immense shaking up from the very foundation of the House.

Lara's first thought was an earthquake. She had never been in one, but what else could this possibly be? She scrambled for a place of safety—but as she ran, she realized nothing she could see through the window was moving.

It wasn't an earthquake, it was her House.

"Are you okay?" she asked, feeling ridiculous when something was so clearly not right.

The House gave one more enormous, shattering shudder. Then settled. A long pause. *I am.*

"What was that? Do you know?"

Magic. Powerful. We are alone now.

"Alone?" Lara was adrift.

I feel no other Houses. We are alone.

"Like, the rest of the Unseen World is gone?" Shock in her voice. It was impossible to contemplate. She could not imagine the amount of magic necessary to accomplish such a separation.

Yes. But you are here.

She could feel that the House was calm, pleased. "I . . . okay. Yes. I am. I am."

The finger bones crumbled to powder then scattered on the wind. That piece of the spell, gone.

Sydney had hidden what she had done at Shadows from Dahlia but started this spell loudly on purpose. This was magic that was impossible to ignore. She wanted the attention of the magicians focused on their Houses, not on anything else, but also, she wanted, here, now, at the end, for them to be inescapably reminded of what their Houses were built on. Of where the source of their power was. That they had made a world and anchored it in death.

Sydney could feel the pull of the magic now, as she stood at the center of the Unseen World and dismantled it. It tried to reconnect itself, it reached for other pieces of its spell. She felt like she was being taken apart as well, like someone had hooked their fingers beneath her bones and was pulling them sideways.

The weight of what she had unwoven was beginning to

destabilize the spell. Magic was no longer in balance. It was in tilt and sliding toward free fall.

That had been precisely what had gone wrong at the end of the Turning. The vacuum of power Miles Merlin had created had so unbalanced things that the separation of the Unseen World from the magic of the House of Shadows threatened the existence of magic altogether. That free fall had turned into an avalanche. This time, Sydney would hold the balance.

Her shadow wrapped around her tightly, the pressure of its magic bracing her against what she had done, what she still must do.

She began the next part of the spell, stepping out of her shoes so that her feet met the ground directly. She stretched her arms to the sky, mimicking root and branch. The scents of green and earth filled the air, and all around her, hundreds of trees with bones in their hearts pulled themselves up from the soil and began to walk.

It sounded like a storm, like thunder, and the ground shook beneath their strength as they moved. They took themselves toward the center of the park, toward the reservoir, toward the place they had all been killed for their magic. A walking forest, a living vengeance.

Dahlia hadn't left the island at the end of the challenge. Mia had been a mistake, clearly. That sort of responsibility, commitment too much to ask from someone outside the Unseen

World. The girl hadn't had the capacity to truly understand how things worked.

Mia had been a mistake, yes, but the House of Shadows wasn't. Perhaps it was time that she finally took it over. There were other ways than a challenge to remake the Unseen World.

The House's door had remained open after the challenge had ended. Her footsteps echoed as she walked through it. It felt particularly empty.

The evidence of Mia's time there remained—a thin and ratty blanket heaped in a corner, pieces of spells scrawled on walls and floors, some even in ink. The filth and stench of occupation. A waste. She had wasted so much time, so much magic on that girl. On all of Laurent's students.

That was her fault. Magic required true sacrifice, not some lesser substitution.

She reached for the House, to check the state of its magic.

Nothing.

Which was not completely unexpected. There had been signs that the House had started to bond with Mia. Cutting her off from magic might have convinced it to withdraw, to hide and wait for safety.

Dahlia reached again, stretching further this time. There was still magic on the island, she could tell, so it shouldn't be too difficult to awaken it in the House.

And again, it felt like she was reaching into a blank nothing, an empty space.

She considered for a moment, then did a quick spell, carving an *x* into the wall of the House. Her magic worked; it could affect the physical House. So something else was wrong. Something that seemed to be inherent in the House itself, as if somehow it was a place that could no longer hold magic. That shouldn't be possible. Unless . . . "Oh, that *bitch*."

A rattle, then, like falling pebbles, in the wall. A tremble, quiet, beneath her feet.

A twig, pushing through the wall and the top of the *x*. A leaf, unfurling greenly from it.

Dahlia stepped back.

And then: a roar. An explosion of green and leaf and tree. Up from the floors and out of the walls and everywhere, everywhere falling white petals. The entire building remade, reclaimed.

The bone trees had returned to the House of Shadows.

Dahlia turned and ran for the door. The trees were faster. They grew throughout the building and in a ring around it, fast enough that in minutes it looked like the House, the island had been abandoned and untouched for decades, if not longer. They took it down piece by piece, separating stone from stone, sending their roots through all of it. A living barrier against that magic ever reconnecting.

Dahlia did not make it off the island. She, too, was taken apart, her bones mingled with all of the others who had died there, held in the roots of the trees.

Sydney felt the weight of the spell more now, a pulling in her joints, the spin and whirl of vertigo. But even so, she permitted herself a grin at the next piece of magic. She conjured fire and ignited the founding documents of the Unseen World. Multicolored sparks shot and flared like fireworks. The spells woven into words and ink and paper, gone. With no other piece of magic to anchor them, to support them, the flame alone was enough to end the magic that had been so carefully crafted. She'd have to tell Harper that lighting it on fire had been a key part after all.

As the pages burned, Sydney pushed on the flames, extending them, burning out the pathways of magic they had held in place all these years.

The flames consumed and then went out.

The world shifted once more beneath her feet, this time correcting itself as the imbalance of magic disappeared. Enough—nearly all—of the spell gone now.

She had wondered if it would feel like an absence. So much gone. But if it was an absence, it was an absence of something that never should have been. Her shadow unfurled, draping itself around her.

The sun prismed through the waters of the Bethesda Fountain, scattering rainbows. The statue once again whole. Sydney turned her face to the mist, to the brightness, and then left. She had a promise to keep.

What remained was the archives. Sydney had known it, when they spoke, and the archives, who had once been Olivia Prospero, had confirmed this.

She had explained: "The excantation won't be complete, Sydney. Not so long as I remain. I am the last piece of the spell that held the Unseen World together, and I am the thing that will bring it back, again and again. Like the House of Shadows. Like your magic. I was made to be neutral, to preserve. But the spell was a living thing—*is* a living thing, so long as I remain—and neutral means a return to the status quo, to the previous balance.

"The House of Shadows has become too embedded in the Unseen World to not be part of that balance. If I am here, it will always try to come back, and there will always be a way for it to do so.

"I am no longer truly an I. I am now too many pieces of spells that wove themselves in through the gaps in what we created when we founded the Unseen World. I am a collective, an archives, not Olivia.

"And I am tired, and would be done. End the spell, Sydney. End me, too."

"You're certain?" Sydney had asked.

"Yes. I'm certain. You'll know what to do."

The elevator ride happened without issue. There was no need for the stored spells—the archives were waiting for her.

In the center of the room, a white candle burned.

Sydney could feel the archives waiting. Could feel the weight of time in the space, the weight of so much magic, the effort of keeping it in balance. She would want to rest, too. "Thank you."

There was no response. She hadn't expected one.

Sydney walked over to the candle and cupped her hand behind the flame. "Exeunt," she said, and blew it out.

CHAPTER THIRTY-TWO

In the end, almost everything had gone according to plan.

Sydney and Mia sat on the back porch of what had been Verenice's house, the cooling remains of a margherita pizza Laurent had made on the table between them. Verenice had left her house to Sydney, and the choice to move in, to stay, had been a surprisingly easy one.

Sydney liked having the pieces of the life Verenice had built for herself around her. It was a way of maintaining their connection. And as much as she had come to appreciate—to care for—House Prospero, that was Grace's home now. Even had it not been, Sydney knew there would always be too many tricky associations for it to ever be hers. This place was, and it made her happy to be able to share it.

"I don't see the point of this spell. Mr. B never even taught it to us." Mia glanced back at the house, as if Laurent might emerge to offer her solidarity. "He said there wasn't a point, when we had electricity."

Mia had come out of the Juliet spell unable to do magic. It was there; she just couldn't access it. She had decided she wanted Sydney to help.

"Which, maybe that's weird?" Mia had said. "Since you're the one who put the spell on me in the first place. But from what I've heard, you're better at magic than anyone. Mr. B talks about you like you're some kind of god. Which means that if there's anyone who can teach me to get my magic back, it's you. Plus, like, he said that you had this problem for a while, too. So you know how it is."

"I do know," Sydney had said. "So I'll do whatever I can to help."

Sydney poured more lemonade into deep-blue glasses for them. "In terms of what you want to choose to use magic for, that's a good point. For some things, modern technology is the better, easier choice. For others, like this pizza, there's a difference in quality. What Laurent makes by hand tastes better than the same thing made by magic, his or anyone else's.

"But in terms of using magic for the sake of magic, there's a reason we start by lighting a candle. It's focus, precision, will."

"Those things are in any spell." Mia looked everywhere except at the unlit candle. When she'd first asked Sydney for help, she'd admitted that she wasn't even sure if she wanted to be able to do magic again. "Like, maybe this isn't supposed to be something for me."

"Did you like magic?" Sydney had asked.

"I loved it. Until. You know. Everything was so wrong."

"This is entirely your choice. So if you don't want to do this, we won't. If you change your mind at any point, we stop. Or you can say no now, and change your mind to yes in six months. Or whenever."

"I think I want to. I think I miss it. I don't think I want it to be gone."

This was their first lesson.

Sydney nodded. "You're right. When magic is done well, all those things are there. But the thing about lighting a candle—calling a flame from nowhere—is that the spell is an illumination. It is a way of seeing. If you're going to be a magician, you need to see things differently than you would as a mundane person."

"This is what you did, to get your magic back?"

"It is."

"Fine, then." Mia concentrated, leaning forward in her seat, her muscles so tense that Sydney's shoulders ached in sympathy, and said the word to spark the spell.

Nothing happened.

She tried again. "What am I doing wrong?"

"Nothing," Sydney said. "Nothing that I can see or sense."

Mia slumped. "I hate this."

"I know. I did, too."

"Did you ever want to quit? Being a magician, I mean. Just have a normal life. You wouldn't have had magic, but you also wouldn't have been caught up in this stuff."

"I never knew how to have a normal life. That was never

an option for me. I was given to Shadows just after I was born. I've lived outside of it for less than a year. I knew nothing outside of magic."

"That's pretty fucked up," Mia said.

"It is. So I wouldn't have made anything except a fucked-up choice. You have a life outside of magic, and from what I know, it's a good one. You can make a better choice."

"All right." She tried—and failed—again. "Can't we try something else? I really, really hate this stupid candle."

"Have you been able to cast any spell, anything at all?"

"No."

"Then we start here."

"Do you have to sit here and watch me fail?"

"I don't. I'll be inside if you need me."

Laurent was standing near the back window, watching Mia. "Is she making any progress at all?"

"Not yet. I don't know if she will or not."

"Is there a time limit on these things? Like, you'll know her magic isn't coming back if she still can't light a candle in a month?"

"I think Mia is the time limit," Sydney said. "And I think that's as it should be. Have any of your other students come back to class?"

"A couple," he said. "Most not. I can't say I blame them. 'Sorry, but you need to go hide from the woman who you trusted so she can't suck out all your magic and incidentally probably kill you' really isn't a message that makes people enthused. But I've let them know that I'm not going anywhere, and that they can come back whenever they're ready."

Many people in the Unseen World were going elsewhere. With the Houses broken, the magic that connected them to each other severed, there was no reason to stay, to concentrate power in one place. Sydney hadn't been sorry to see any of them leave.

"Does it feel finished to you this time, Syd?"

"No. I don't think it ever will be, not really. The magic? Sure. I ended the spells. They're done. They can't come back, not the same ones anyway. That part I know. But the people that made the Unseen World? That part doesn't go away. It won't."

"Well, that's fucking bleak."

"I don't know," Sydney said. "I think maybe it just is. Magic, or its lack, doesn't change anything fundamental."

"True."

"Hey, Mr. B, I've got to go." Mia slid the door closed behind her. "I promised Uncle Raúl I'd walk Meatball with him."

"Sounds good."

"Did you light the candle?" Sydney asked.

"Not yet. But maybe I could come back next week."

"That would be good."

"Cool. See you then."

After they left, Sydney sat at the same table, in front of the candle. The shadows from the garden stretched over where she sat, offering respite from the day's heat. Her own shadow joined with them, indistinguishable from the others, its weight bearable now, its magic, regardless of source, entirely her own.

It was the simplest spell. The first she had learned, the one that had never left her. It was also magic, impossible and strange. She spoke a word.

ACKNOWLEDGMENTS

Thank you to Adrienne Celt, who was the first person to make me seriously think that I could write a sequel to *An Unkindness of Magicians*.

Thank you to Dessa, for writing a song that was the perfect thing to listen to approximately one million times while writing this book, and for generously allowing me to quote from the lyrics.

Thanks go to Dahlia Adler for letting me borrow her name for what was—at the time—a fairly minor character, and then for allowing me to continue to do so when I checked back in and said, "Um, maybe she's evil?" All I borrowed was the name—actual human Dahlia is terrific.

Fran Wilde and Martin Cahill offered thoughtful feedback on various drafts, and this is a better book because of that. I wrote many pieces of many drafts during Jami Attenberg's #1000WordsofSummer, and was grateful for that internet presence.

It takes a number of people to turn a pile of words into a real book. Thank you to my fantastic and brilliant agent, Alexandra Levick. I am so lucky to have her in my corner.

This book also benefited from the expertise of Brianne Johnson. Thank you to my editor, Joe Monti, in particular for his patience and for never making me feel rushed. Vault49 provided another stunning cover. Thank you to Madeleine Maby for returning to narrate the audiobook. Brian Luster was a terrific and thorough copy editor. Thank you to Cassidy Sattler and Tyrinne Lewis in publicity and marketing. Thanks also to Jéla Lewter and everyone else at Saga.

Writing this book was the most difficult thing I have done in my professional life. I could not have gotten through it without the support of my friends and loved ones. Aside from those already named, my thanks go to Megan Kurashige, Maria Dahvana Headley, Mike Chen, Guy Gavriel Kay, Neil Gaiman, Bill Schafer, Amy Kennedy, Jen Miller, Becky Krug, Nicole Saharsky, and, as always, to my family.